Barry and The Chronicles

Barry and The Chronicles

By Alun Davies

Published by Valley Boy Ltd

ISBN 978-1-9997855-0-5

Printed in the UK

www.barryandthechronicles.com

Contents

If there is a dedication to this book then let it be,

"Words can deceive you
They come and they leave you
They're just a sound
That you may
Like to hear"

If there is a purpose to this book then let it be,

"Set peace free"

If gratitude is due then let it be,

"To those who have helped in the finalisation of this book when they know who they are"

However to my family, both present and future, I need only say.......

"You are all and everything."

Alun Davies, December 2017

The Start is at the Beginning

No **one** knows much about Spiders. People think they do, but actually they don't. To help put this right I shall explain something of the real Spider world by telling you the amazing story of Barry, a small Spider born in London.

Firstly, there are three Spider facts you must remember. These are important in order to understand what happens to Barry and how he came to change the world forever.

About one in a million and one **Spiders** has special powers. It isn't clear why these Spiders are chosen and it's not really important. They are known as "Secrets" because no one is sure who they are. From time to time there are unexplained events that can give rise to certain suspicions in the local community, but that's as far as it goes.

Next, Spiders can talk, although they're never normally heard by anyone except other Spiders. The sound they make is very strange and confusing and cannot be recognised by normal ears. It's like listening to a dog barking, a car horn and a piano playing at the same time. That's hard to imagine, don't you think? No wonder we all refuse to accept combinations like that and ask yourself, no matter how many you've seen, have you ever heard a Spider?

Finally, they live under a strict set of teachings called "The Chronicles", covering different subjects and aspects of life. These originated many years ago and have served the Spider world very well. Perhaps the most useful lesson to learn from them is that Spiders should never forget how wonderful it is to be a Spider and means they are the happiest, friendliest and most useful of creatures. The Spider Chronicles form the central thread throughout this story because they are the source of all Spider wisdom.

Although Barry was a young Spider he quickly realised he was a Secret. The main reason was that he could understand what every creature said. It didn't matter if it were a horse or a human, Barry knew what they were saying. You'd think this was a useful skill to have at your disposal, but it made Barry realise how unhappy the world could be unless an effort was made to enjoy the beauty we all share; everyone and everything is so special. Also, Barry could make things happen, things that were impossible to explain.

In the house and garden where Barry lived there were of course other Spiders. Usually they kept themselves to themselves unless there was a need to come together to discuss something important. There were the daily pleasantries if one Spider happened to meet another but normally Spiders prefer to be alone; a Spider likes everyone but likes themselves best.

However sometimes talking was needed and Barry was the most useful Spider to go along and represent the views of the neighbourhood. That's why he was at the local

Doctor's surgery where, under the stairs leading to the storeroom, a very important matter was on the agenda!

All Spiders knew that when they were seen, people seemed afraid. This was hard for them to understand when they had no thought of hurting or scaring anyone, but the very sight of a Spider was certainly causing uproar. They were being caught, thrown outside, washed down sinks, sucked up in various machines or even worse. This was becoming a big problem and the meeting had been called to discuss what could be done about it.

"People don't like us because of our webs," offered Bobbin miserably. He lived in the broom cupboard and hated any sort of problem. "We leave them behind and sometimes they get in the way of others. Let's face it, we can be a bit untidy."

"It's not that," said Frankie (Spiders only need one name). "It's because no one hears us and so we can't tell people how nice we are."

"Well, if you ask me, people are stupid, and there's nothing we can do about it," said a wise old Spider called Arthur. "That's always been the same and no different now. This whole meeting is a complete waste of time because I don't see how the problem can be solved."

The talking went on much longer but just went round and round in circles, as many such discussions often do. Barry said nothing but this was a problem he had known about for a while. He knew why people were afraid of Spiders, but he also realised that if he explained it to everyone there would be mass panic because it struck at the very core of being a Spider. So he only spoke to say how the matter needed much more thought. Everyone agreed and it was decided to reconvene after 14 days and start over again.

Barry's knowledge on the subject started when he was listening to his people-family talking about having a picnic. It sounded such fun that he thought he might go along. The change of scenery would do him good and he could easily hide in the rugs they would be taking. Spiders often adopt a family to live with and share their home, causing no trouble. Indeed, as you will see in later chapters, a Spider can play a big and important part in family life.

"Where shall we go?" said Mother, who was a **lovely** kind person and, like most mothers, always wanted what would be best for others.

"I don't mind," said Father, who left such decisions well alone.

"Please can we go by the river?" said Daisy. She was a pleasant enough five-year-old who liked exploring and always wanted to be doing things. She was often close to Barry because of that but she didn't know; Barry was able to keep so still he could be practically invisible.

Anyway, a lovely family day out looked in prospect, but Jessica now had her say. She was 15 years old and didn't like the countryside or the river, or anything except playing video games and spending time on her computer.

"If we must go anywhere then please not by the river," she said. "It's a horrible place, full of creepy crawlies and ants that get everywhere."

Barry thought Jessica was very silly to think "creepy crawlies" (whatever they were) would have the slightest intention of bothering her but it was the next thing she said that really shocked him.

"Then there are Spiders to consider. I hate them. Their long legs hurrying and scuttling about – urgggh – horrible."

In a moment it had become clear. One of the greatest things about Spiders was actually causing the difficulty – their legs! Since then, Barry had noticed such misplaced thinking many times; in fact he was so used to it that he stayed extra-motionless around people. It seemed that the worst thing he could do was move; it was much easier to blend into the scenery and not be seen at all.

Anyway, Jessica's intervention had meant there was no picnic by the river. It showed Barry how easily a better outcome can sometimes become unavailable through trying to satisfy the view of a minority.

So after the Spider meeting, Barry had much to consider. Clearly the difficulty had grown into a major issue and, as a Secret, he should try and fix it. The question was, how?

I have already explained that Barry was still young, but already he possessed great wisdom because he was aware of the truly important things in life; I'm sure you know of these already. Spiders are made aware of them through reading The Chronicles, but because some of those teachings are to be reflected later in the following chapters, I shall say no more about them at this stage; simply remember that all true treasures must be found, not gifted.

In any case, I should return to the problem of "legs" and the solution Barry put in place.

Well let's see, his people-family often invited friends to their house for dinner and Barry sometimes hung around listening to the conversations, even if he often became bored when nobody was saying anything of interest. Nonetheless, he looked forward to those evenings because after they'd finished there were occasionally spilt drinks to discover and Barry had a great liking for cider, as did the Father of the house. Both of them were of course far too clever to drink much of it, but for Barry a little tiny sip and no more, if it could be found, was a real treat.

That was how he came to be in the middle of the kitchen floor early one morning a few days after the meeting. There had been a noisy party the previous evening and Barry was having a very small taste of cider from a spill not yet cleared away. Then Mother came in and saw him! Barry knew mothers are kind so he wasn't worried about being flushed down a plug-hole or anything really nasty like that; it was just one of those strange times when he suddenly knew he should be seen with his legs on full display. As you will learn later there is always a moment to be what you are meant to be. Later Barry couldn't help but laugh to himself when he thought about Mother screaming and running upstairs to tell Father she had seen a Spider drinking cider.

He also kept thinking why did he allow himself to be so visible? Normally he would have stayed extra motionless, but there was just something in the air where his usual caution wasn't necessary. Then he suddenly knew why and in an instant his plan to correct a fear of Spiders took shape.

"Maybe they aren't so very different from the rest of us," he heard Father saying later at breakfast, "but I've never heard about a Spider drinking cider before."

"It was actually really nice to see in a funny sort of way," said Mother. "He wasn't scary or anything, even though he had those long legs that usually make me shiver, but they weren't hairy legs and I could just tell he wasn't going to cause any harm or try to frighten me."

She suddenly looked down on the floor, "Where do you think he is now?"

"He's here somewhere," said Father, and of course he was right.

"Urggggh, Spiders," said Jessica, also looking around.

Barry knew it was time to bring his secret powers into play and so right there and then he planted a thought in Mother's mind. It was that she should leave another drop of cider in the kitchen, just to see what might happen. Sure enough the next morning there it was, with Mother peeking from behind the door leading towards the living room.

Barry slowly approached the cider. Then he sang a Magic Song he had written for the occasion and allowed Mother to hear and understand it. This had never happened before in the entire history of Spider Land, but Barry knew the problem of Spider legs was all caused by a feeling that cannot be properly explained. It was a fear of the unknown, or to describe it in a slightly different way, a fear of something you don't know about. He was sure the song would solve things.

Mother came from behind the door and studied him carefully. Barry didn't move but watched her approach. After a single sip of cider he walked slowly away (Spiders never crawl) and vanished out of sight. His plan was under way.

Over the next few days Barry took an extra keen interest in the family and made sure he heard everything Mother was saying. It was soon clear he had made a big impression.

"He was singing, I tell you," said Mother. "He let me hear. It was all about his legs."

The family were roaring with laughter.

"Spiders don't sing, they can't sing. It must be your imagination," Father smiled indulgently.

"Just because you've not heard a Spider singing proves nothing," Mother said stubbornly. She knew what she had heard.

It was time for the next part of the plan. When Father went to work and the children had gone to school, Barry boldly appeared in front of her. She didn't seem at all afraid and simply stopped what she was doing and listened carefully in case he sang again. Barry concentrated hard and do you know what happened? Instead of screaming, Mother started singing the Magic Song.

Barry smiled to himself; the plan had worked.

Music is a very special means of communication. Sometimes, just sometimes, you hear a few bars of a song and can't stop it going over and over in your head. Perhaps you don't even like it, but it won't go away. The song Barry had let Mother hear was like that, but especially powerful because it was written as a Magic Song. When you heard it you couldn't help but sing it and learn from it. Barry knew the song would affect the whole family, but even he didn't know how big the repercussions would be.

Yet I must not get ahead of myself in the story of Barry's life.

Very soon, Father, Jessica and Daisy could all be heard singing the Magic Song.

"It's about Spiders you know," said Mother. "The Spider in the kitchen sang me the song so I would understand there was no need to be afraid. Their legs are just how they move because it's how they're made."

It was now time for the ultimate test. Barry went to Jessica's room and waited. She came in and there he was, on top of her bed plain to see. For a moment they looked at each other in silence and then she started singing the Magic Song, knowing there was nothing to fear. She had realised it was silly to be afraid of something that caused no harm.

The Magic Song continued to spread far and wide. It went way beyond the family because, as I told you, when you heard it you had to start singing it.

So when it came to the next meeting in Spider Land there was nothing to discuss.

"I don't know what's happened," said Arthur, "but for some reason people seem much happier to see me. They've stopped running away and are actually a lot more friendly."

The other Spiders agreed and everyone went home. Barry said nothing because, like him, it was all a secret.

Have you heard the Magic Song yet? No? Well, don't worry, it's still spreading so very likely you soon will. Then you'll understand some other things to help you later when I tell you more about Barry and his adventures.

2. Problems and Solutions

"Show me the web and I'll show you the Spider!" It was something Barry often said when explaining how everyone does things in their own way. No two webs were the same and, likewise, different creatures made, described and tried to solve problems differently.

The responsibility of understanding problems and finding their solutions had recently become more relevant to Barry in his life as a Secret. You have already heard how Barry wrote a Magic Song to solve a fear but it was not only within his own people-family that he needed to fix things.

The Chronicles stated that problems would inevitably arise and then explained why they are not all easily settled. It just wasn't likely that one viewpoint was 100 per cent right and the other 100 per cent wrong; the truth was probably somewhere in the middle, with good arguments on both sides. Yet this could make it difficult to find a solution, so it was a complicated situation. However, the important thing stayed the same, and that was to find a way to settle all disputes quickly and easily, once and for all. Therefore, the total number of available solutions could never be reduced, only increased, and each was equally important.

A replacement solution was now needed in the part of Spider Land where Barry lived, and he was the one who needed to find it.

Let me explain what happened.

An old tree had blown over in a storm, but for many years it had been used as a solution. The parties to a dispute were each allocated a side of the trunk and the next creature passing by, on one side or the other, determined matters. You will realise that the answer rested on the approach taken. Different outcomes were possible when they depended upon a direction of travel and this was considered to be of great merit in finding a solution. Judgement was final and the issue settled there and then. This simple means of solving a problem, right or left, was accepted as being more important than right or wrong.

It may seem a strange way of doing things, but isn't it better than fighting or shouting, with the outcome resting on who is the cleverest, strongest, biggest or loudest? Settlements arising from such sources were unacceptable and regarded as totally inadequate by Spiders, although when emotions were running high, such wise judgement could sometimes be forgotten.

So although Barry was often faced with an issue where a number of solutions were possible, he knew that the key thing was to find an answer readily accepted by the parties involved. A fair, available and obvious approach was usually the best way for individual differences to come together.

You see, the fact is that differences are not a problem. It was a subject Barry knew a lot about because he was not like other

Spiders. For one thing he didn't like heights and always tried to stay on the ground. Neither would he simply just hang around waiting for things to happen, but preferred to see what was going on by patrolling downstairs in the house and the surrounding gardens. It meant he could keep an eye on developments affecting different creatures in the neighbourhood, and was there to help make things better when it was time to do so. He didn't have many close friends because he was never still for long enough, but because all Spiders like their own company best it didn't matter much.

But the differences about Barry didn't stop there. As a Secret he had been given responsibilities and magic powers, so the replacement of a solution was for him to sort out. No one else would understand but later, as he looked out of the kitchen window at the activity under way, he thought to himself that two days is a very long time in the life of a Secret Spider.

You see, a number of events had just taken place.

Near the bottom of the garden in the house where his people-family lived stood an old shed and in it lived three Spiders. The first was Emery. His real name was Henry but everyone called him Emery for reasons that will become obvious. The second Spider was Sinbad, who had been born in a caravan and still often went away, travelling far and wide. Finally, there was Splash who, unusually for Spiders, loved rain and jumping around in puddles.

They all shared the same problem. An entire army of ants lived in and around the garden and because a shed was full of interesting things to explore, it meant that ants and Spiders were often very close together, creating a problem between residents and visitors.

"It just won't do," said Emery. "They're getting everywhere."

Sinbad agreed. "I don't mind anyone going wandering but they should respect the fact that we were here first. Why do they stay in the shed for so long poking into this and that? I wonder they don't get bored and go look somewhere else."

Splash wasn't happy either. "Only yesterday I counted 50 or so ants shuffling about next to me. It's not right. This is our home and they're not welcome!"

"The Chronicles are no help. They're useless for this sort of thing. It's all very well explaining how Spiders should be helpful and friendly but ants don't know anything about The Chronicles, and as far as I can see they're not interested in solutions, just in causing problems," bemoaned Sinbad.

The three of them discussed matters for a long time, round and round and round, before deciding to do something that was always the most obvious thing to do.

"I'll go and ask Barry about it," said Emery. "He usually knows what's for the best."

So the very next morning that's what he did.

"It's not that we don't like ants, Barry. It's more the fact that they get everywhere, and there are hundreds of them. They don't seem to need any privacy, and hang around even more than we do. Anyway, the long and the short of it is that we don't want them in our shed." Emery was happy to get matters off his chest and was getting himself quite worked up over the whole thing.

This was why he was called Emery, he was unfortunately by nature a bit aggressive and it is, of course, no way to behave.

"We can't use The Chronicles when we're faced with a problem of ants who aren't interested in solutions," he said.

Barry listened quietly. Spiders never interrupted each other, something that was considered to be extremely ill mannered, and instead he waited patiently until Emery had finished.

"I understand it's a problem but there are two things. Remember that The Chronicles always apply and so they must have the answer; sometimes it's just not obvious. Then, you're wrong to say ants aren't interested in solutions because every creature must be. All we need do is find how a solution can apply; it's not always easy."

Barry could never say too much in case he gave away the fact that he was a Secret. So it was a case of seeming to be helpful, but without providing answers; in the world of people it was sometimes called politics.

"Well, that's not moving us forward very far, is it?" said Emery. "You're saying The Chronicles apply when we can't see how, and ants are a reasonable enough bunch when we know they're not! What am I supposed to ask the others to make of that?"

"Tell them all problems can be seen," said Barry, "but until you are ready to find them, solutions remain hidden."
Then, that evening Barry heard his people -family talking. Father was saying, "I think our garden shed is in the wrong place. I've always thought it would be so much better nearer the house. Walking too far down that slippery path when it's dark or raining can be dangerous and a bit of

a pain; even bringing me a nice cup of tea when I'm working in there seems difficult."

He smiled at Mother as he said it, knowing how well she looked after him and the family.

She ignored the remark anyway and said as far as she was concerned the shed could go completely.

"It's falling apart and totally useless," she said. "The only time you go in there is when you want some peace and quiet so there's no point you claiming otherwise about somewhere to pot the garden plants or whatever. I'm not even sure we need a shed; the garage is perfectly adequate for storage space. We never put the car in there, do we?"

Father didn't like the sound of that very much. "Well actually, I do need somewhere to pot the plants and tinker about; I like seeing something grow and develop. I'm in there quite a bit with one thing and another, even if sometimes it's just for some peace and quiet. Let's think about it, shall we?"

Barry had noticed that when there was no obvious agreement, Father usually said, "Let's think about it" as a way not to find a solution. It didn't seem a very sensible approach to him but he didn't want to interfere with such family affairs. On a personal level, he'd much prefer the shed to stay where it was, at the bottom of the garden, well away from the house. Too many Spiders crowded together can cause difficulties but we needn't talk about all that in this particular story.

So Barry now had three things to consider. The need to find a new solution for Spider Land, the residents and visitors issue in the garden shed and the prospect of losing some of his own privacy.

This is how he fixed things.

Early the next morning he went into the garden to see the ants. They had a very odd means of communication involving their antennae and much shuffling about but as a Secret, Barry understood them perfectly and could make them understand him. Most gardens were inhabited by different ant tribes and were governed through local commanders. If he gave a message to any one of them it would be told to all.

He found a large ant about to squeeze between some rotting planks at the back of the shed. For an instant they just looked at each other before Barry explained what would be happening and what he wanted the ants to do. They were a perceptive enough bunch, who gave Barry a great deal of respect and always took what he had to say very seriously.

Then he went back into the house to see Mother and planted some thoughts in her mind before returning to the garden to see Emery, Sinbad and Splash.

"I was thinking about the problem with the ants. I knew the solution was in The Chronicles, and I think I've found it."

"Well, tell us," said Sinbad.

Barry gave a spidery sort of grin. "I can't say in advance because then it won't apply, but I'm pretty confident that soon the ants won't trouble you in the shed any longer."

"Hummmph, I want to know what's happening," said Emery. "Why should you know something we don't? It's our home after all."

"Just be patient. What I need you to do, a little later today, is go visiting or exploring; just be somewhere else."

Barry added a few more details and walked quickly back to the kitchen leaving no chance to ask further questions. Emery, Sinbad and Splash were baffled but excited – Spiders love solutions.

Mother had spent the late morning on the telephone.

"Good, that's all sorted," she thought.

She had been to look at the garden shed and, on opening the door to see inside, was shocked to see the number of ants in there. It was very alarming because she had the idea they might soon overflow into her house, something that wouldn't do at all.

Later in the afternoon, the pest control man arrived from the Council and rang the doorbell.

"Thanks for coming so quickly. Let me show you the problem," said Mother. The man followed her through the house and down the back garden path. She opened the door to the shed and pointed inside with a grand gesture.

"There," she said.

The man went in and looked around. "Where?" he asked.

"What do you mean – where?" replied Mother impatiently.

"I can't see any ants," muttered the man poking about, "just a few old Spider webs."

Mother peered in; no ants could be seen.

"They were there before," she said lamely. "Hundreds."

"Maybe," said the man, "but they're not here now so there's nothing for me to do," and he went back to the Town Hall.

Barry and some of the ants were watching all this from behind a plant pot a few feet away.

"Let that be a lesson to everyone," Barry told them. "To misuse anyone's home by overstaying a welcome is a bad thing to do; every home is a precious place that deserves respect."

A little while earlier Barry had told the ant commander to announce, at a large meeting called in the garden shed, that a man from the pest control department of the Council would be coming there later in the day. He would spray everything with a deadly chemical if he saw any ants at all and so they must stay clear of the place for a few hours. In a separate private discussion the local commander had agreed that, to remove the risk of such future visits, the ants would stay out of the garden shed as much as possible.

Of course Barry had arranged that Mother should open the garden shed door when the meeting was underway.

"It was very odd," Mother told the family. "In the morning there were loads of ants and in the afternoon they were gone, but don't think this alters anything. The garden shed is falling down, it's dangerous and has to go."

"That's just what I've been saying," said Father. "It should be nearer the house."

"Oh no, it's not coming nearer here," she said, thinking again about the possibility of ants in her kitchen, "but we can get a new bigger one, and we must all make better use of it."

Barry had made sure Mother was keenly aware that ants would soon be inside the house in large numbers given any sort of opportunity.

So a new shed was delivered for the same spot at the bottom of the garden; the old one had been cleared away. It was a nice new home for Emery, Sinbad and Splash, staying pretty much free of ants, and Barry kept his privacy. Finally, when a problem appeared, a replacement solution for Spider Land stayed quick, simple and relatively unchanged: would the next ant passing by the new shed do so on the right or the left? Of course it still depended on the direction of travel.

Barry explained to everyone how Paragraph 17 of Chapter 4 in The Chronicles helped him fix things.

"If a problem cannot be solved it is only because the time is not right for the solution to appear, but there is more than timing to consider. Because every solution is related it cannot be found from within a position of self-interest, so consider yourself as the difficulty before looking elsewhere."

You should note that this is the first of twelve specific Chronicle paragraphs I shall bring to your attention as Barry's adventures continue.

Anyway, for the moment, Barry had solved everything that needed to be solved because the solution suited everyone.

3.
A Christmas Story
(Jessica's Dream)

It is now time for you to fully realise the part a Spider like Barry plays in the life of a people-family, and this tale will explain it and remind you of the unseen influences that m ay have shaped your own development. Then perhaps you should take a moment to consider them.

Barry loved Christmas. He remembered the smell of pine coming from the tree and the air of youthful excitement Jessica and Daisy always brought to the occasion. He even liked snow because by pressing down a little harder with his legs he found he could make interesting patterns in the garden when he was patrolling around. He especially liked lots of visitors coming to the house for dinner parties because Barry was a very nosey Spider and enjoyed the various conversations. No one knew he was there, of course, but when the subject was particularly interesting or somehow affected Spider Land, he'd join in by planting a thought in someone's mind as if it was their own opinion.

However, Barry also felt Christmas should be more than an opportunity to eat, drink and be merry. It was a time for remembering that the important things in life are those we often fail to appreciate. After all, why should people prepare to be thoughtful and kind just at Christmas?

So Barry wished that Christmas would mean to everyone what it meant to him. When he thought about it, the same message kept coming into his head; peace on earth would be the best present we could exchange. He had the image of peace being an idea somehow caught and imprisoned in a cage; the world would be a much better place if it could somehow be released.

"We should set peace free," he thought.

None of that mattered to the children of the house. Five-year-old Daisy naturally considered Christmas as the time to eat nice things, stay up a little later and think about all the presents Father Christmas would bring in response to the list she'd prepared. Jessica, being 15, had developed a different view. It involved trying to look much older than she was and going to a party where neither Mother or Father appeared.

At that moment, however, Jessica had something else on her mind because on her way home from school she'd found a fat wallet crammed full of money, credit cards and so on with contact details of the owner, who was surely a wealthy businessman. It was perhaps money saved up for the festive season in order to buy presents for loved ones; who knows?

Jessica understood that the right thing to do was return the wallet but she had been with a group of fellow school pupils when it was found. A bigger girl, who was not one of Jessica's close friends, had actually snatched the wallet from her hand and taken £50 for herself before she gave it back. So even if Jessica returned it there would be less money for the rightful owner and possibly some tricky questions to answer.

Unaware of these events, nothing but Christmas was on Daisy's mind and in particular there was the item at the top of her wish list of presents, a new bicycle. Unfortunately, Mother and Father had reluctantly decided that because money was in short supply that year they couldn't afford it.

"I'm sorry, but we can't spend the same pound twice," Father had said.

Jessica knew how much Daisy wanted that bicycle and thought it would now be easy to buy it. She did actually wrestle with the possibility, but the next morning she had decided what to do. After adding £50 of her own pocket money saved for Christmas she handed the wallet over at the local police station.

Jessica was brought up in a good family home. That's the first thing to say really because in such circumstances the chances are much higher that you can learn how best to behave. Yet even without such influence you will still grow up aware of right and wrong because deep down in everyone each of those possibilities can be found.

The Chronicles covered the situation very early in their teachings at Chapter 1 Paragraph 3.

"By itself nothing is bad and nothing is good. If that were the case there would be isolation but both are connected so it cannot be. The issue is always your environment and the opportunity it creates, because although all threads of influence can be stretched to breaking they can never be broken. It is time that moves and not the face it displays upon."

Barry read The Chronicles, as did every other Spider, but there was a strange aspect about it for him and it grew deeper every time he turned a page. He thought it must be a feeling shared by all Secrets because of the added responsibilities they had been given. His insight was not exactly wrong, just underestimated as you will see. No other Spiders were quite like Barry.

At any rate Barry had been well aware of Daisy's Christmas list and all the events involving Jessica. This was his family and as usual he wanted to help so he planted a dream in her head. It wasn't necessarily true that anything different would have occurred if he had stayed out of things but a strong image and recollection can often serve as an example to show what should be done.

This is Jessica's dream:

There were three monkeys living together in a jungle full of animals that would be happy to eat them. The common danger meant the monkeys knew each other very well; after all, they were the only monkeys in that jungle. In the middle of it was a long, deep and wide river and one day the monkeys found themselves trapped on the riverbank and faced by a large hungry lion. They could not go

*forward or sideways and the river was behind them so there seemed
no escape.*

*The lion was thinking how well he would eat that night. He
knew he could catch one of the monkeys even though it would give a
chance for the other two to escape.*

*The monkeys looked at each other. They were thinking
the same as the lion: if one of them was caught, two could get
away, but who would be caught?*

*The first monkey was the biggest. He felt there would be more of
him to eat and so he was certain the lion would want him for dinner. He
said to the other two monkeys the lion wouldn't be interested in them.*

*The second monkey was the tallest. He also felt there would be
more of him to eat because of his height. He said he'd be the monkey
on whom the lion would like to feast.*

*The third monkey was the oldest. He had lived a long time
and, through experience, knew many things. He said not to worry
because by looking after each other, none of them would be eaten and
he told them what to do.*

*The lion got nearer and nearer. Two of the monkeys stood still
but one of them walked forwards. He explained to the lion that
by looking closely he would be able to tell who would make the best
meal, then he'd know the monkey to catch.*

"How will I know that?" asked the lion.

*"Because monkeys eat bananas, they have yellow eyes if they're
nice and healthy. The one whose eyes are very yellow will therefore
taste better," said the first monkey.*

"Well then, let me look into your eyes," said the lion. "Hmmm,

they look brown to me.”

“Yes,” said the monkey, “but the others have eyes of bright yellow.”

“Very well,” growled the lion. He thought to himself there were still had two monkeys left so his dinner was safe even if the first monkey was not telling the whole truth.

“You can go,” he said. The monkey quickly disappeared into the jungle and safety.

The second monkey walked towards the lion.

The lion looked into the monkey’s eyes; they were indeed very yellow. “So, you are my meal,” he said. However the monkey replied, “Why would you eat a monkey with yellow eyes? Everyone knows that yellow eyes are a sign of old age and so I wouldn’t taste very good at all.”

The lion now considered matters much more carefully. “I can see for certain that you are old; string and bones really. That last monkey by the riverbank does look much tastier, so you can go as well.”

The old monkey headed for the jungle and safety.

The last monkey had watched the others disappear into the jungle, and then he turned and swam across the river.

The dream means different things depending on when it is being considered and whether you are single like the lion or able to work together with others, like the monkeys. The lion was being all he could be but the monkeys were being what they could become. As Barry’s adventures unfold you will see the increased opportunities available with co-operation.

For Jessica, the dream had given her something else to consider. The tall monkey who was able to swim could always have escaped and left the other two monkeys to their fate, but instead he acted with the others to achieve the greatest benefit. The old monkey had acquired wisdom and knew what to do in the best interests of them all, even though he was never likely to be a preferred dinner! The biggest monkey was prepared to be the first to approach the lion and place himself in the immediate and greatest danger.

There were other lessons from the dream such as realising that an opportunity cannot easily be put aside thinking another will come along shortly; in time they stop coming. Also the lion didn't think that monkeys could swim because he'd never seen it happen, but that didn't mean it couldn't be done. The unexpected often happens and is to be treated as that to be expected; thus it is a surprise to find a wallet but a reaction can be prepared. Indeed, if you think about it, I expect you can find even more to consider; every dream carries much potential.

On Christmas morning the family had gathered bright and early to open all their presents; although there were plenty of lovely things for Daisy there was no bicycle.

Hiding her disappointment as much as possible, Daisy **thought**, "It doesn't matter," but deep down she was very sad. Of course Barry was there, watching and waiting; he had made some preparations of his own.

A knock came on the door; standing outside was a large policeman.

"Is this where Daisy Davies lives?" he inquired.

"Yes, but why?" asked Father.

"Because there was a reward for anyone who provided information leading to the recovery of a wallet lost in Victoria Park, and we thought at the station how it would be nice to hand it over on this particular morning. A nice Christmas present, eh?"

"I still don't understand what it's got to do with Daisy," puzzled Father.

"She was the one who found it," answered the policeman. "A teenage girl gave it in to us but said Daisy Davies of this address had found it and asked her to hand it over because she was going to be passing by the station. As far as we and the rightful owner are concerned, Daisy is entitled to the full reward. No one else is involved, the teenage girl left no details, so the reward must be for Daisy. Happy Christmas and tell her well done!" He turned and walked away, leaving a generous cheque for £500 with Father!

Mother and Father found the whole business quite remarkable and were still talking about it long after Christmas.

"It really was a strange situation, don't you think?" said Mother.

"Yes, for sure," agreed Father, "because Daisy knew nothing about it. Naturally we both thought Jessica must have been involved somehow but when I asked her she started talking about monkeys, lions, the greater good and the need to think of others. I couldn't get any more out of her than that so I still can't make sense of it."

"Well, the money certainly helped us sort a few things out. It's as if it was meant to be. After all we couldn't have done more to try and give the reward back. We went to the police station with Daisy who said she hadn't found anything but the policeman seemed unable to listen through that nasty cough he had. He told us to accept the reward because it was meant to be that way. What else could we do? Throw it away? It allowed us to buy Daisy a bicycle and Jessica would only accept £50 from it so we had some money left over to help pay some bills. Everything worked out perfectly," said Mother.

Barry was listening. There were some things that, as a Secret, he couldn't explain to anyone. In particular he was proud of Jessica who had decided not only to return the wallet but also to make up the shortfall with her own money. The reward was in the action she took. The bicycle for Daisy was merely part of the reaction Barry had prepared; you will learn much more about these things later.

You may also like to know that the girl who had snatched the wallet from Jessica and taken £50 for herself did not enjoy Christmas. Remember that there is a price to pay for pleasure founded on the pain or suffering of others.

The Chronicles covered the point at paragraph 8 of Chapter 1:

> *"It is wise to look beyond the immediate and ask if you are worthy of all you enjoy, because nothing can hide you from yourself or what you deserve. Were that possible it would serve little and deny much. Two masters will live hard together when one yields nothing and the other requires reflection."*

It all meant that Barry's message of Christmas had spread a

little more widely.

"What could be a better present?" he thought to himself.

This marks the point where Barry's life took on a new dimension and what happened next is faithfully recorded in the following pages. However, before reaching this important moment you should know that he had already been in lots of other adventures and experiences. Only three of them have been told so far; perhaps one day you will hear of others.

4.

Barry Comes of Age

It was time to learn more about the wider world. The first thing was that Barry received a message.

"I need your help, please come quickly." It was signed "Martin."

Barry had long suspected that there was a fellow Secret Spider living nearby. Some strange stories had been circulating and in them Barry could detect certain interventions of a Secret kind.

A further sign of a Secret was that Charlie the cat delivered the message. Secrets can understand and communicate with all creatures, but because cats can speedily roam far and wide they are in theory the best of messengers. Unfortunately, they are very unreliable and if Martin could cause a cat to do something it said much for his talents.

Having another Secret to hand wasn't a problem as such. Secrets, as with all Spiders, much prefer to keep themselves to themselves and Barry wasn't too bothered about Martin as long as he stayed on his own patch. However, then came the message. Barry was at first inclined to ignore it; after all he had plenty to do in keeping an eye on things within his own people-family and the local community. Yet he quickly realised that, in keeping with the general Secret code as laid down in The Chronicles, he had to respond.

In any case, Barry was by nature extremely curious. What could possibly be the reason why his help was needed, and how did Martin even know he was a Secret? The whole business needed to be investigated further.

When necessary, Spiders can travel around by shooting a thin layer of web up into the sky and letting the wind take them to where they want to go; it is just a case of holding onto the thread until reaching the intended destination. So Barry soon found himself in a garden several hundred or so houses away where he set about locating Martin. This last part was a little more difficult because it was quite a big garden and Barry was a stranger. Moreover, he was an unwelcome stranger as far as the resident community of ants were concerned; they carefully guarded their territory from intruders.

"Shove off," said a large local inhabitant, blocking his way along the path.

Barry frowned. He wasn't used to being spoken to so rudely and didn't care for it much, but he couldn't explain matters without indicating that he was a Secret (that would never do), and so he made a sharp right turn into the grass where he soon found … more ants.

"Who are you?" asked one of them, eyeing him suspiciously "Ants really do get absolutely everywhere", Barry thought to himself. In consequence they usually know what's happening.

"Er, how are things around here?" he asked.

"Who wants to know?" came a reply.

"Oh, I just wondered," said Barry ignoring the question. "Actually, I was just passing by and thought I'd take a look for myself. I'd heard it was a nice place to live."

"Well it's not, so be on your way," and the ants strode off so quickly Barry wondered if something had alarmed them.

Yet everything appeared nice and quiet, and so Barry carefully started to explore. At one end of the garden was a collection of gnomes looking as if they'd stood guard on the spot for a hundred years. Alongside them was a sizeable vegetable patch where someone had once obviously spent long hours weeding and planting; at one time cabbages, tomatoes and potatoes had all thrived.

Next was a child's swing, carefully installed on a bright green but somewhat overgrown lawn except that the lowest point underneath the seat was worn bare of grass by the feet that had rubbed the earth dry. Then there was a patio area; on it stood a table and a few chairs where clearly the resident people-family had spent summer evenings with their children.

At first glance, the house looked like all the other houses Barry had seen but yet there was something odd about it. Barry couldn't quite identify what, but it was unmistakable. He stood and stared, and thought and thought, and walked round the front and sides. Finally, the reason became clear; the house had a strange eerie doorknocker and it cast a shadow everywhere. It was unlike anything Barry had ever seen. It was circular in shape but in the middle was something that looked like a cooking pot and seemed to have a life of its own because it wasn't connected to anything for support. Little beads of bubble like steam appeared to be rising from within the pot, only to disappear when they reached the inner circle edge.

It was certainly an unusual thing to see on a door. Barry stood and looked at it for quite a while, trying to come to terms with all his senses and instincts that were giving him a warning sign to stay well away.

"Thanks for coming. You must be Barry."

Barry turned and saw a Spider who was small but somehow gave the impression of being much bigger. There was authority in his voice when he said, "Come with me, we can't stay here in the open!" Barry instinctively knew this was Martin.

They entered the empty house via an air vent. The silence inside was strange for Barry in comparison to his own noisy home and he wondered about the children who had once lived there.

"You're not what I expected," said Martin looking at him closely.

"Why? What did you expect?" asked Barry.

Martin stared at him. "Hmmm, well never mind that, it's good to meet you. I expect you want to know why I asked you to come along."

"Of course," said Barry, who had decided to say very little until matters had clarified.

"This was a happy home until a short while ago. The people-family who lived here were a pleasure to be around and every creature in the house was made to feel welcome and safe. Mind you, that feeling didn't necessarily extend beyond the walls," Martin grimaced.

"Let me explain. As you know every home develops a bit differently. Here, we called our community inside the house the "Domestics" and those in the garden were known as the "Outsiders". Some of them were a funny bunch; there was always an argument going on, usually involving the garden ants who had no regard whatsoever for The Chronicles. Frankly they were often unreachable and my role here became a sort of peace officer simply trying to maintain some sort of co-existence. It really was very difficult. You may have heard some tales about that but I needn't dwell on them right now because it doesn't help."

All of this was related in a calm matter-of-fact sort of way, but then Martin became more and more agitated.

"Then she came," he said, "and it all got much worse. I don't know why my people-family would have thought it necessary, but they advertised for someone to help with all the cleaning and hired a woman called Mrs McGaw who turned out to be," and Martin lowered his voice to a whisper, "a Witch!" Little did Barry realise at that moment how his life would never be the same again.

Martin continued, "Of course, I could tell straight away. An evil atmosphere entered the house, but what could I do? As time went by she poisoned everything that had been good. Domestics started to disappear, then my people-family started arguing, the children became unhappy and cried a lot, even the flowers and plants in the garden began to die. I did what I could and managed to stop some of the worst of it but it was a constant struggle. Mrs McGaw realised there was something in the house working against her and she set out to find it. Before too long she had tracked me down; she had some powerful abilities that were hard to defend against, especially when there were fewer and fewer creatures left for her to investigate. She clearly knew all about Secret Spiders and began to concentrate on finding me."

Barry thought to himself that if Secrets are so well known to Witches, then where did that leave him? Still, the main thing right now was to understand everything Martin was saying.

"Soon I was the only one left in the house and I needed to go into the garden and live alongside the Outsiders who, I can tell you, were not that keen on the idea because it brought extra attention on them. However, the pattern stayed just the same. Creatures kept disappearing. Some Spiders first, then all the others (except the ants of course who don't take much notice of anything unless it suits them), and the garden became unfriendly, lonely and a no-go area for the family."

Barry listened intently. All of this was clearly very bad news but why was the house empty of people?

Martin continued, "Before long she had everything under her control and could progress to the next stage of her plan. Witches try and capture the minds of some little children so they can also be trained as Witches, just like them. Of course, I couldn't let that happen so I came out of hiding and used some powers to go back into the house and plant certain thoughts in the minds of Mother and Father. I wasn't able to tell them anything directly because people wouldn't believe this sort of thing goes on, but I could get them thinking how maybe a long holiday or a fresh start elsewhere would be a good thing to do. I just needed something that would give me time to get things sorted."

He continued, "I had to make sure they didn't tell Mrs McGaw about this until it was all arranged so I placed certain restrictions on their conversations for as long as I could. You will know this takes a lot out of a Secret. I was left quite exhausted, and so some of my defences and concentration levels were down. This gave her the opportunity she was waiting for and the next stage of her plan then became clear. Other Witches started to come to the house and I learned their intention was to begin a whole community of Witches right here. So not only were my people-family and all the creatures in the house and garden under threat but potentially the danger would spread for miles around, maybe even to your place."

Barry suddenly felt an evil wind blow through the house. Martin felt it too and fell silent.

"Sssssh," Martin whispered. "She's coming; we need to concentrate and combine our powers."

Barry and Martin joined forces and made themselves invisible and unnoticeable. The cold wind blew around the room, into every corner, but it could not see or touch the two Spiders, who remained "Secret."

After a while, it exited through a closed window. Barry had never experienced anything like this before and couldn't help but realise how all his senses were at a full level of excitement and anticipation.

Martin said, "Notice how dry and clammy cold it has become? When a Witch is close at hand, the temperature drops. Anyway, where was I?"

"You were explaining how the house came to be empty because your people-family went away, but that doesn't tell me why you've asked me here."

"Because I need more Secret Spider powers to settle matters," answered Martin. "I would have thought it was obvious," he added.

"How did you know I was a Secret?" asked Barry.

"The Magic Song. That one about **our** legs! Stroke of genius! It got everywhere, with everyone singing it. I knew it had to come from a Secret and it wasn't difficult to trace it back to your house." Barry thought things over. "Let's go into the garden, I don't like it in here," he said.

They found a spot near the vegetable patch and snuggled down to discuss what they should do.

As usual, the immediate issue was to deal with the inquisitive ants soon on the scene.

"Who's your friend?" they asked Martin nodding towards Barry. "We've become used to seeing you out here but all the other Spiders have left and we don't know this one."

"It's none of your business," said Martin. "Look, I don't have time for all this right now so leave us alone if you know what's good for you." Barry noticed that with those last few words Martin seemed to grow bigger.

Clever, he thought. Certainly the ants must have thought so because they disappeared towards the gnomes.

"How did you do that?" asked Barry.

"Oh, so there are still Secret powers you haven't mastered yet are there? Well, don't worry about it, you're still young. Over time and with a little practice you'll find you can do more and more," replied Martin, who was obviously pleased at the chance to impress and continued in a rather conspiratorial manner.

"Although if you read The Chronicles carefully you'll see they explain why some Spiders never reach their full potential. It's the same with all creatures, of course, so it applies equally to Secrets, but for some reason I somehow don't think it will apply to you. Anyway, in balance there is a prophecy told of a Spider still to come who develops beyond us all. I suppose we're all waiting for that to happen because there's so much more to be done, but never mind about it now, here's what we should do."

Looking back on things Barry realised it was the first time he began to understand what it meant to be a Secret and how the responsibilities of the position extended way beyond his people-family. The wide variety of powers Secrets had been granted could not be used narrowly when there were so many deserving causes needing their attention. Good must always confront evil and when it does, then good will prevail because it is the stronger force. If evil is to triumph, good must do nothing.

Co-operation with others is also essential because no single creature achieves as much individually as a group working as one. It was something Barry knew already and you may also remember this point because it featured in Jessica's dream; the best lessons are taught over and over again.

Martin had also hinted that The Chronicles needed to be studied for many years before you could find and apply all their teachings. For instance, paragraph 48 in Chapter 3 covering "Work, Leisure, Influence and Responsibility" now seemed much more meaningful.

"Spiders come in many shapes and sizes but in order to remain the happiest, friendliest and most useful of creatures some must have due recognition of events in and beyond Spider Land. They cannot ignore any developments threatening the existence or wellbeing of other creatures. Such Spiders are best placed and equipped to help where needed and on them together will rest a special duty."

Barry fully appreciated he was one of those Spiders on whom the responsibility rested. He had come to "help where needed" and was ready to do more.

Matters resolved quickly with Martin's plan. So much so that when his people-family returned from their holiday, the house had been restored to full working order. Domestics and Outsiders were on the best of terms and the garden was looking healthier than ever. There was no sign of Mrs McGaw.

It had been simple. Martin knew, not just that the Witches were cold but, fundamentally, how they needed to be cold, and I shall have to explain more about that in due course. Anyway, acting on this information the two Secrets combined to make the empty house very hot indeed. All heating systems and appliances were turned up to full blast and they used their merged powers to multiply that heat many times over until the place resembled a blast furnace!

The next time Mrs McGaw brought her Witch friends round they were unable to stay there for more than a minute; the Secrets had ensured that the temperature could not be turned down or off. No Witch could stay in that house for very long and, because they had many other ways and many other opportunities to bring their plans into effect, there was no need to remain in any single situation where they could not easily prevail. Of course it meant the battle against the Witches was merely being transferred elsewhere, but Secrets remain vigilant and ever on guard.

Afterwards it was also easy for the Secrets to adjust the heating system controls backwards so that no extra costs became a burden to the family. Creatures soon reoccupy living space and in the best of the weather the plants in the garden re-established themselves and quickly began to thrive. The family returned refreshed to a house where once again they would be happy.

Barry knew his life had changed forever. He'd found a new Secret friend and discovered there was an evil force of Witches in the land. He also realised that it was his duty with others to fight against them whenever and wherever they appeared. There was much to learn and, before returning home, he held a very long conversation with Martin about all things connected with being a Secret Spider. You will hear more about that later.

Back home, and listening to little Daisy laughing upstairs, he particularly wanted to always try his very best to keep everyone, and especially all children, safe and sound.

"It's good to be a Secret," thought Barry.

The Passing Time Game
(Mother's Speech)

Barry would never neglect any situation where he could help but, although still trying to come to terms with the things he had learnt from Martin, always took a special interest in people. He felt that many creatures have the ability to teach, but people have the most to learn. This is a story to illustrate the point.

Barry had noticed, at the dinner parties his people-family liked to host, that everyone could talk but few could listen. Time and time again questions were politely asked with absolutely no interest in a reply. People competed for the space to say something without realising that no one then cared what was said. Talking was an exercise in passing time while waiting for a better opportunity to come along, even though it never did. Still worse, it meant the potential of the moment was lost forever.

There is a similarity here with a thrown away photograph, an instant never to be recaptured. The real sadness being that others are denied the chance to see what was once worthy of note to someone. In much the same way, Barry realised that conversation was often simply an excuse allowing time to pass by until the next thing happens; words mean nothing when talking matters more than listening.

"If only people could read The Chronicles," he thought, "they would understand it's foolish to think the life changing words are those spoken; in fact it's those that are heard".

As a Secret Spider, Barry had the ability to concentrate very hard on what was being said and would never ask a question if he had no interest in the reply; that would be very rude! It was why all creatures liked speaking to him, because he made them feel interesting and special. Not everything can always be important but everything seemed important when talking to Barry and the result was that he knew many things. You should remember that, when absorbing information, you are gaining the great gift of understanding.

Now, by way of some further background to this story, every weekend Barry had developed the habit of going to the local park with Mother and Daisy. He liked the fresh air, and a patrol around his own garden could get a little boring. There was always much more happening in those open spaces and Barry was, as I keep saying, a very nosey Spider. From such innocent beginnings began the tale of Mother's speech.

At the park, a particularly noisy mallard called Jeremy was telling everyone within earshot about the news that the Government proposed to build a railway line, straight through the middle of the duck pond.

"What will it mean for us?" quacked a little fellow called Spencer.

Jeremy shook his head. "Obviously it's not good," he answered grimly. "As far as I can make out there is such opposition from some wealthy householders about building the railway line anywhere near their own gardens that the idea is to build it through this park and drain our pond instead. Perhaps it's not such a big deal for those of us who are independent and pretty mobile; we can find somewhere else to live but it will hit those two hard." He nodded towards a pair of fine swans on the opposite side of the water.

"Oh dear," said a moorhen called Sophie. "Yes, it would be a shame for them."

"I don't see why," commented Stretch who was a goose with a very long neck. "What's so special about two swans?"

"You move around so much you've got no sense of time and tradition," Jeremy replied somewhat dismissively, "but Joe, the male swan, has been in this park for years. This is where his roots are and it's where he belongs. He's getting on a bit now and I doubt he'd want, or be able, to go anywhere else."

"It's very sad of course but I still don't see … " began Stretch. "He was with another swan before," explained Jeremy, "Sylvia was her name as I recall, but unfortunately she was run over by a car. Joe saw it happen; broke his heart. Took him a long time to get over. I've heard that if a male swan loses a mate he spends the rest of his life looking for her. Anyway, I suppose because he saw the accident happen it didn't apply, because he found a new love called Emily."

Stretch turned his head. On the far side of the pond he could see both swans swimming together. They seemed to have no thought in the world but each other and, on looking more closely, a young baby swan was paddling between them.

"Joe's going nowhere. I know him too well. Emily's younger and, like us, could perhaps start again somewhere else but she won't go without Joe," continued Jeremy, "and you may have noticed that they've just had a baby swan; a lovely little cygnet called Tracey. What would happen to her if the railway comes?"

Barry heard all this and didn't like it. Loyalty was his favourite quality and he loved the way swans committed themselves to sticking together through thick and thin. So he felt unhappy to learn that Joe and Emily might be forced to separate and Tracey looked so content that he couldn't bear to think of her in any distress.

Apart from the swans, Barry was also well aware that the park was a major benefit to everyone who lived in the neighbourhood. There was a real need to have a facility at hand where all creatures nearby could share in, and be surrounded by, greenery. He decided he'd find out some more about the planned railway and set about using his powers to undertake some speedy research.

The next day he planted some thoughts in Mother's mind.

"It's a pity the railway line is planning to go through the park, don't you think?" she asked Father innocently. "I noticed yesterday how many people were using it."

Father barely looked up from the football page in his newspaper and gave a sort of grunt by way of reply.

"So, what do you think?" Mother persisted.

"What about?" he said.

"About the park and the railway line. Do you listen to anything?"

"What am I supposed to say?" Father said after giving the matter some brief thought. "We're told that progress requires a railway and so a railway is what we're going to get. People will simply need to find somewhere else to walk the dog or whatever."

Mother persisted, "But what if it's not progress because it's not what the people want?"

"It doesn't matter what you call it," said Father. "Look, this is the way it works: those in power decide what will get them re-elected to power. They know that everything cannot be unanimously agreed so they go for those things that a majority will support, or at least will do nothing much about; that's what happens. You may not like the railway but others clearly do and someone, somewhere will be making money from the whole thing."

Mother wasn't happy. "It's not that I don't like railways, it's that I like parks, and so do plenty of others. Marion takes Jonathan to the swings nearly every day; the local football team plays there on a weekend and trains in the week; it's where lots of people go running and walking; it's a place to meet. That's some examples even before we think about the birds and all the wildlife. I was looking at the ducks and swans only yesterday. Surely it's our park and we should say what happens?"

"It's our park up to a point but then it becomes the Government's park; that's what I'm trying to tell you. They have to consult us about the plan but really it's usually already settled by then. I've seen it all before. There was a time when what the people said actually mattered but those days are gone and now we have new rules of the game."

Mother looked very unhappy about it all.

Father hated to see her like that so after a moment he added, "Tell you what, the next public meeting to discuss this proposal is tomorrow evening at the Town Hall. If you feel so exercised about the whole thing, go along."

"You know, I think I will," said Mother.

"And so will I," thought Barry, who was listening.

Mother felt very strongly that building a railway through Victoria Park would be a big mistake and wanted to say so. However, she was fully aware of the need to consider very carefully what she should say at the meeting. It wasn't just about turning up, she wanted to make a difference.

"This is a case where there's no point going just to hear others speak. I do want to hear what they've got to say but then I'm going to put my point of view, and I want people to listen," she thought.

Yet the prospect of addressing the meeting worried her a lot. Standing up in front of a packed meeting, most of whom she would not know, and making some sort of speech was very scary. She decided to write an outline so that at least she would have notes to follow; mumbling along and turning bright red would be her biggest nightmare.

"There won't be an excuse to dry up and be unable to say a single word if I have a script I can follow," she thought.

So that evening she settled down to write. She typed a suitable heading, "Why we need to keep Victoria Park." After a few moments of thought she underlined it twice, but that was the extent of her progress. No other words appeared and the longer she waited for further inspiration the more panic she started to feel.

"Oh dear," she said to Father, "I want to say something that will make a difference and make people really listen but I can't find the right words. This is something very important to me but others may not feel the same way."

"Don't worry," Father replied sympathetically. "The people at the meeting should be interested; that's why they attend in the first place and I'm sure you'll get a lot of support. What's the worst that can happen? Every heartache disappears you know, but I'm sure they'll get the message."

"Do you really think so? I do hope you're right. I'll try to write something again after doing the shopping in the morning," Mother said.

As she slept, Barry planted thoughts and confidence in her mind and the next day words flowed onto the paper.

Father drove Mother to the Town Hall.

"I'm not letting you do this all by yourself," he said, and smiled with encouragement.

They found seats at the back; the room was crowded. There were two local Councillors on the stage with representatives from the railway alongside Arnold Pugh, who was the Member of Parliament for the constituency. He sat in the middle and was clearly chairing the meeting.

"Order, order," he shouted in best Parliamentary fashion and the room hushed.

The head railwayman explained why the new line was needed and said that of course they would be taking as much care as possible so as not to spoil the environment beyond what was absolutely necessary.

The Councillors in turn explained their reluctant consent to the plan because, although far from perfect, they had been told it was the best option. They had issued information papers locally calling for comment but had received few meaningful replies. This meeting was the last chance for people to have their say on the proposal.

Mr Pugh then explained why, from a central Government point of view, it was a good idea. He droned on and on, but after a short while very few were listening. Finally, at long last, he asked if anyone from the audience wanted to say something.

Barry was there. It was always easy to hitch a ride in the family car and from the car park to the Town Hall was only a short distance; he could easily travel it by web-thread.

Once inside he had settled down. As you may have expected, Barry had firstly ensured that Father read about the meeting, then he had helped Mother with the script; yet that wasn't enough. He knew all about people talking with no one listening; when Mother spoke it wasn't going to be like that.

You may recall from an earlier story that Martin told Barry how Secret Spiders have powers that Barry, who was still very young, didn't even know about. Since then he had been practising every day, discovering more and more of the things he could do; much was becoming possible. Barry, like all of us, simply had to believe in the possibilities.

He quickly cast a wide, receptive web-spell over the meeting. The room was quiet and attentive when Mother stood up to speak; everyone was prepared and willing to listen.

She cleared her throat; Father squeezed her hand.

"I don't usually do this sort of thing," she began, clutching her script tightly, "but from time to time there are occasions when you can't stay quiet and say nothing; this is one of them. Victoria Park is important. I dare say that a new railway line is important too but it's not important for the ducks and swans, it's not important to the trees, it's not important to the flowers and frankly it's not so important to me. I'm sure many other people feel the same way."

The room was hushed.

She continued, "I use the park every week, I take my daughter there to see the birds and feed the ducks and when I'm there I hear laughter, I see people exercising, talking to each other, looking and learning. Not about great works of philosophy or literature, but about the little routine things that are the cement in everyone's lives; they are learning about nature and they're learning to be together. There is more to life than hustle and bustle, money and profit. My daughter Daisy is nearly six and I want her to know that."

The meeting was still really quiet, everyone was attentive and Mother didn't need to look at her script.

"Victoria Park gives us, all of us, an insight to a better world. It's not buildings and cars, banks or money. It's somewhere offering something we cannot take away from others because it was given to us and belongs to children like Daisy.

"Hear, hear," shouted Father, determined to be supportive. Mother paused and looked around at the faces.

"Is there really no alternative to destroying something precious? Cannot the railway be re-routed elsewhere so that our open green spaces are preserved as much as possible for us to enjoy? If we all object then, with the help of Mr Pugh, I'm sure another way can be found. I gather that the railway company had no requirement to build in any particular place; they do what the Government tells them to do. Neither is the Government completely sure about this plan. They have been through these issues before with new airports and new roads. Things can change and they have been changed. The Government just needs to listen to the people and do as they're told."

Everyone in the room applauded and cheered. Mother was slightly embarrassed; she could feel herself starting to turn red but had nearly finished.

"One more thing. The Councillors and Government we elect may grow so complacent as to think they can tell us what to do. They're wrong! We always have the power; we simply need to use it. Only the people matter. There must of course be an acceptance of responsibility for decisions made on our behalf but that's only when those decisions are truly made on our behalf and not on behalf of others. If that's not happening then we must elect different representatives into office."

Mother looked meaningfully at Mr Pugh and sat down to more loud applause and cheering.

"Well done," said Father. "I wasn't sure you had that in you."

"Me neither," she said.

Mr Pugh stood up and cleared his throat. After the noise had died down he began to speak.

"There's much in what the lady says. I grew up around here and played in Victoria Park." His throat suddenly started to tickle and he gave a cough, then another and another. "Nonetheless, the plain fact is that (cough, cough, cough) the Government has carefully examined…" Mr Pugh felt his throat getting more and more irritated. He took a drink of water… "every aspect of the proposal and there is no doubt that," and he paused for a few seconds as if wrestling with his own voice, "the best thing to do will be to let me take matters back to my Committee. The interim proposals on the railway were not passed unanimously. Hopefully there's something we can do to change the decision and given the strength of feeling expressed here tonight, I think there must be."

That is what Mr Pugh said, but it was not what he wanted to say. He had stood up with the intention of gently rubbishing Mother's speech and pointing out the economic arguments as to why the railway needed to be built, and why they had decided it should be built through Victoria Park. Yet, for some strange reason, he heard himself saying something completely different.

He sat down with a puzzled expression on his face.

On the journey home Barry wondered if all the lessons available that evening were understood by those at the meeting;

he doubted it. His experiences observing people had taught him much about the "passing time game". It was the reason he had made sure that everyone in the audience listened carefully to what Mother was saying.

At least he knew Victoria Park would now be safe and that Daisy could continue feeding the ducks; moreover Joe, Emily and Tracey could stay together in their happy home. He'd also successfully, for the second time in these stories, used one of his Secret powers to make people cough; his confidence was growing.

The Chronicles constantly indicated that acting for the good of others always made you feel good about yourself. It was so inherent that it never needed to be specifically stated in a paragraph spelling it out. So at home, when he heard Mother chatting happily to Father and putting on the kettle for a nice cup of tea, Barry had every reason to feel satisfied with himself, but then suddenly his whole body shivered.

He knew what it meant; a Witch was coming!

6.
Trust and the Learning Process

Everyone older than you has been your age. It means your parents have an advantage in being able to look backwards for longer, remembering things you cannot yet know, so when they are willing and able to offer some guidance you must seek it and listen carefully. Spiders don't have parents as a source of information so they gather it where they can; it explains why The Chronicles play such a big part in their society.

However, Secrets are different from ordinary Spiders because of the powers they were specifically given to be used for the good of other creatures, so they hear more, see more and know more.

Barry was still thinking a lot about Martin and trying to recall every word he'd said. Older Secrets were the best source of reliable information about Witches, and Barry needed to know everything possible. His senses confirmed that the time was fast approaching when it would be necessary.

In another part of London, Mr Pugh was telling his wife what had happened at the meeting.

"It was the strangest thing I can ever remember. I just can't understand it. I stood up to say one thing and heard myself saying something else."

"What exactly happened?" asked Mrs Pugh.

"Well, the meeting started and everything was going along nicely. Councillor Green said his bit and I said all the usual things about why the new railway line was needed to enable economic and industrial progress; nothing about the profits of course. Then there was some of the stuff about trying to keep all the consequent disturbance and upheaval to a bare minimum – again all routine. You know the tactic when I speak, try and bore everyone to tears and lose them in facts and figures. Finally, after a while I asked if anyone in the audience wanted to say something – naturally hoping no one would – but this lady stood up and started talking about recreation, trees and wildlife; honestly, you could have heard a pin drop. Then it was about understanding how there was more to life than money and that people were meant to keep a protective eye on all the creatures of the earth. As if that wasn't enough, she brought her daughter into it saying there was some sort of promise implicitly made to children that the world we leave them will be better than the world we were given. She did speak very well; even I had to listen. The whole room was in rapt attention, cheering her on."

Mrs Pugh was staring at him intently. "What happened then?" she said.

"Well, that's about it, really. I stood up to say why all those well-meaning sentiments counted for nothing against economic reality, only to find that I actually said she had made some excellent points and we'd need to look at the whole thing again. I just can't understand it, but there's no going back now on a promise I've made in a public meeting. As you know, many people on the Committee weren't at all happy about the plan to dig up the Park; now they'll have the opportunity to change everything and I think they will."

"I see," she muttered. "What about your cough and the lady who did the talking, do you know her?"

"I don't know about the coughing. I couldn't stop when I was going to say something in support of building the railway but didn't cough if I was agreeing with what the lady was saying, and I do know her actually but only through her husband, William Davies. He works for the Council as a Senior Engineer on the Road Safety Team. They've got a couple of kids – live over Louvain Terrace way."

"How old are their children?" asked Mrs Pugh.

"Oh, I don't know for sure. Two girls, I seem to recall, one about ten years older than the other," he replied. Mrs Pugh looked very thoughtful.

The very next day she could be seen wandering along Louvain Terrace. When school finished, it wasn't hard to spot Jessica and Daisy walking up the road and going into Number 14.

Mrs Pugh waited a while and then walked boldly up the front path and knocked on the door; Mother opened it.

"Yes, can I help you?" she said.

Mrs Pugh looked at her carefully and sniffed the air. "Oh, no, not really, um, you may not have noticed me but I was at the meeting and heard you speak about Victoria Park. I simply had to come and tell you … very well done! If only more people would speak up for their rights and for their children then the world would be a far better place."

"It was nothing much," said Mother. "I felt I had to say something and the words just came out!"

"Really?" answered Mrs Pugh. "How wonderful, and what a gift." She smiled a thin smile.

"Anyway, I must be going. I only called by to sing your praises." In a moment she had turned and, with one final sniff, was gone.

Mother shut the door and walked back into the kitchen. Barry had been in the hallway listening; she saw him waiting, but of course because of the Magic Song, she wasn't afraid any more.

"I wonder how that lady knew where I lived?" Mother thought aloud. "Through the girls I expect."

Barry knew the answer, and he didn't like it.

Mrs Pugh returned to the apartment she and Mr Pugh rented. It was at ground level of an old Edwardian house in Balham; two more apartments were overhead. Mrs Pugh liked living there because the ground floor also owned the garden and from time to time it was a useful place to send Mr Pugh. That wasn't necessary now because he was away on Parliamentary business. She went to a cupboard and pulled out a bulky tome invisible to all but the intended reader, called the *Witches Reference Book*. She turned to somewhere deep inside the pages. You may already have guessed that she was also a Witch, just like Mrs McGaw.

Meanwhile, after Mrs Pugh's visit to Louvain Terrace, Barry was considering all kinds of strategies to keep his family safe, but couldn't decide on the best one. He could only think about innocent little children being turned into Witches.

"That's not happening to Daisy!" he thought. She was his main concern.

Eventually Barry decided he should involve others in the local community to form some kind of defence force. He thought about the shed Spiders like Emery, Sinbad and Splash, and perhaps they could have some involvement, but when it came down to it he knew what was needed.

Wandering into the garden, Barry soon found the resource he had identified. I shall come back to their part in all this shortly.

Firstly, I must explain that Barry's overall thinking had been heavily influenced by the things Martin had explained about Witches. It started with the fact that they were extremely crafty and could easily hide themselves away by behaving just like everyone else; it was soon obvious that there was clearly much **more** to learn. For instance, they couldn't stay anywhere hot for long as a result of a Spider spell I have previously promised to explain and soon will. They didn't like being cold either, even though they could make others feel very cold indeed, and in fact freeze them. Also, to reach their maximum powers, they needed to be with other Witches because their combined force was much more effective than that generated by a single Witch. It was just like the Secrets, as you will have noted when Martin asked for Barry's help in concentrating their strengths together.

However, Martin had also told Barry something else, something quite extraordinary! He explained that there were some Spiders who had extra powers and abilities; they were called Super Secrets and were very rare indeed. Over the centuries they had played a massive part in the battle against Witches. Martin gave the example of a daring Super called Derek who had penetrated into the very heart of the underground Witches' kingdom situated somewhere below London. Only there, in the Great Hall where Witches lived when not in the outside world capturing the minds of children, could a certain web-spell be spun against them. Derek had managed to do it, although nobody knew how, spinning a spell to mean that Witches were unable to withstand extreme heat. It wasn't easy because Witches had developed strong defences against many different threats, yet Derek had found a weakness and made use of it. Not much but better than nothing and, as Barry had just discovered from the encounter with Mrs McGaw, the spell came in very useful from time to time.

Naturally, Barry wanted to know more about Derek. What had happened to him? Martin didn't know; he could only say, with a hint of a smile, that Derek had not been seen since going underground.

Barry laughed. It was funny, but he still had questions. For instance, if Derek was alone in the Great Hall and hadn't been seen since then, how did Secrets learn about the heat spell?

Martin said, "It seems the Witches told us."

Barry was puzzled and had further questions but after a while Martin was fed up with explanations and made clear the time wasn't right for more answers. He did add that in due course Barry would learn all he needed to know if he studied The Chronicles. That was where all Spider life was, or would be, explained.

Oh, I nearly forgot to mention that Martin did say something else to remember concerning how to spot a Witch from an ordinary person.

"It's not difficult for Secrets, but very hard for most other creatures and seemingly impossible for people; it's why we have such a special part to play in keeping children safe. The first thing is that you will feel cold even if no one else notices the temperature. Neither is it a normal feeling of cold, it's a dry, wet, clammy feeling unlike anything else you've felt before. You will also feel watched. The Witches know we are their sworn enemies and they've developed a sort of radar system that tells them when a Secret is near. I'm not exactly sure how they do it but it seems to be by smell; they sort of sniff the air. It all means that neither Secrets nor Witches can creep up on each other because, of course, we can always sense if one of them is near."

When Mrs Pugh knocked on the door at Number 14, Barry felt the dry, wet, clammy cold and thought he was being watched more closely than ever before. At least he now knew what it meant.

Speaking of Mrs Pugh, she had also been thinking very hard since visiting Mother and trying to satisfy herself as to whether or not there was a Secret within the house. You see, the Witches had already realised there was one somewhere close to hand because of the Magic Song. It had even been discussed at the last London Witches meeting, and the recent Town Hall experience of

Mr Pugh had been enough to make his wife think that the Secret could be inside Louvain Terrace.

"This is serious," said Mrs Johnston, who was a very successful Witch, famed for the number of children she had recruited.

"No doubt about it," agreed Mrs Crier. "Whoever wrote the Magic Song is extremely powerful. People have started liking Spiders and that puts pressure on all of us. It won't do. Whatever next?"

"I used Spiders as a means to frighten my children targets," said Mrs James. "After they were scared I could make friends and reach into their minds. It was easy then, but it's different now."

Mrs Porter started to speak and the others went quiet. In their command structure she was the London Chief, very ambitious and a thoroughly nasty piece of work.

"You are all idiots," she hissed, "with no idea of the danger we are facing. We are under threat like never before. I had hoped there would be no more Secrets but I heard the Magic Song and now this one called Barry appears; he must be found and dealt with before he develops. He is still very young so we should be able to trap him easily enough once we know for certain where he is. That's the first thing to do; go and search everywhere and don't return until he has been found."

The Witches all trooped out to find Barry.

Mrs Pugh suspected he was in Louvain Terrace but her senses told her she needed to be sure before making any announcements.

She couldn't forget the smell she had noticed there and it filled her with disquiet.

"Was that a Secret or not?" she thought. "I've smelt them before but this wasn't the same. I know there's one somewhere around here for sure because of the Magic Song. I'd never heard anything like that before; I even started singing it myself! Then there was the business about Victoria Park and all that coughing and speech manipulation on poor Mr Pugh, but would a Secret be living in Louvain Terrace and getting involved with plans to build a new railway?"

She felt she needed to know the facts before saying anything. There could certainly be no question of announcing where the new Secret Spider was if he wasn't there. Mrs Porter would be very angry about wasting everyone's time and might even mix a punishment potion for her to drink. Mrs Pugh decided to return to Louvain Terrace and confirm things once and for all. Then she would tell all those who needed to know.

Barry was speaking with the garden ants; these were his favoured local resource to help safeguard Daisy but he was struggling to gain any meaningful co-operation. His thinking had been that with their discipline, knowledge of tunnels and wide coverage they would be ideal for front line observation and protection duties. Unfortunately, although they were, without question, extremely hard working and organised, they were definitely lacking in some ways. With their variety of amazing skills you'd think ants would make more of themselves but somehow it never quite happened. They can certainly do a lot, but always fall short at the final few hurdles where they could make a difference. It was probably because they had no group of extraordinary ants, comparable with Secrets, to drive them forward but there again, nor did other creatures – except perhaps people.

Another problem was that ants never spoke outside their tribe. They would communicate amongst themselves but never co-operated more widely and usually fought when they met others.

"Very uncivilised behaviour," thought Barry.

Nonetheless he needed to quickly find a way to make use of the assets they could provide. His early contact didn't seem to have gone well even though Barry had made relatively minor requests and explained them quickly and clearly. How they then passed that information between themselves was a complicated business and Barry felt no need to explore it further; it was enough to know that they had a working system. The bad thing was that communication was a slow undertaking; receiving any concerted reply would take a while.

All he could do was explain exactly what he wanted; that was simple. The ants should keep an eye on Daisy and tell him immediately if anything out of the ordinary happened.

Over the next few days Barry kept busy, planning other ways of protection. There were all the other Spiders around Louvain Terrace who might be able to help, but Barry needed to keep his powers hidden from them so couldn't really draw undue attention to himself. Eventually, he reluctantly decided that perhaps a short term answer might be cats, and Barry thought he could rely on Charlie to get things under way.

"I like Daisy," said Charlie, "and I could help but as you already know, cats are unreliable. We might do what we say but then again we might not. When it comes down to it every cat, including me, will look after its own interests. I'm sorry to say this but cats are very selfish."

Barry knew it already. "Look Charlie, it hopefully won't be for long; see what you can do. Probably we only need three or four of you and it really is just a question of following Daisy and letting me know if there's a problem. If you help, then you'll be rewarded." Barry thought it was strange he was talking about rewarding cats, yet Charlie seemed satisfied with the promise. It is true, as you may know, that all cats have a highly developed sense of instinct but this seemed like trust on a new level.

"If you say so Barry, then that's fine but all the same, after a short while the boys will still get fed up, bored, and simply wander off. We just can't concentrate for too long on this sort of thing," Charlie said.

Barry also felt he should get Martin involved and asked Charlie to make the contact.

"Tell him I need his help and advice," Barry said.

Anyway, that was the deal. Charlie would try and get some cats to follow Daisy and hopefully within a couple of days the ants would be in place and ready to take over. It wasn't an ideal set of arrangements but it was the best that could be done in the short term.

The next morning Barry watched Jessica and Daisy leave on their way to school, followed by a tabby, furtive-looking cat, keeping a respectable distance away.

"Well done Charlie," Barry thought.

So with everything now in place it was a waiting game until Martin arrived. His experience would be invaluable; Barry still had little practical knowledge of Witches.

He settled down to wait in a dark corner of a cupboard; he wanted some peace and quiet to be alone with his thoughts. The kitchen could get too noisy.

He was constantly on high alert, however, in case he heard a cat or an ant calling his name and the next afternoon, that's exactly what happened. Barry wasn't surprised that events seemed to be moving quickly.

Hurrying outside he found himself faced with a cat he hadn't seen before.

"I'm with Charlie," said the cat. "Come quickly, Daisy's in great danger."

Barry swung himself up onto the cat's back and they were off. There was no time for web-thread travel. Down the road and around a corner, past several streets to right and left, they hared along until reaching a disused warehouse.

"Daisy left school early and went in there," said the cat. "It seemed odd and then some women arrived separately. They went in one by one. Charlie said to get you."

Barry went straight inside without further thought and looked around. He couldn't see Daisy anywhere but parts of the building were very dark so he carefully started looking around. It was quiet and clammy cold; he felt he was being watched. He knew there were Witches nearby but his thoughts were all with Daisy. Then shapes began to appear; he was surrounded.

"Hello, Barry," one of the shapes said to him. "I'm Mrs Porter and I've been looking for you."

The shapes moved closer and Barry realised that Daisy wasn't there and he had been tricked.

"Never rely on a cat again," he told himself grimly. "What a fool I've been. Daisy leaving school early and coming here just doesn't sound right, now I think about it. I've let emotions rule action," and he thought about what The Chronicles would say at his recklessness.

It definitely wasn't looking too good for him at that very moment. The cold was becoming intense and Barry felt like he was being blinded by hundreds of spotlights.

He prepared to summon all his powers and placed a defensive web around his legs. Yet he was finding it hard to do and he realised that more and more hostile cold spells were being placed upon him; he started to feel very weak.

"Freeze him, freeze him," he could hear the Witches chanting.

"Concentrate, Barry," he was telling himself.

Nonetheless he was getting colder and weaker with every second that passed. Suddenly there was a shuffling at his side and he heard a voice.

"Nice to meet you Barry. I'm Derek."

7.
Preparations and Expectations

Barry woke up and looked at Derek and Martin.

"What happened?" he asked.

"You passed out," said Derek. "It was a difficult situation: lots of Witches surrounding a young Spider; bound to be tricky, even hard for an experienced Super. Not just any gathering of Witches either; Mrs Porter was there. She's got plenty of nasty spells, a really bad Witch, and I recognised one or two District Head Witches as well. The London lot were certainly out in force."

"I don't remember," said Barry. "I felt so cold and saw all these shapes around me but after that, nothing."

"Don't worry about it," Derek smiled, and after a pause added, "So you're Barry?"

"Yes, but what happened? I want to know." Barry persisted.

Derek's smile broadened still more. "A typical Secret," he said turning to Martin. "Nosey!"

They both laughed. Barry looked at them and felt himself getting slightly irritated.

"What happened?" he repeated, his voice sounding just a little bit more forceful.

Derek's smile didn't change. "Martin, can you give us a minute or two, please."

After Martin had left Derek continued, "OK, OK. Look, it's not about what happened in the warehouse; it's more since I heard The Magic Song. So, let me see, where to start?"

Derek collected his thoughts; there was a lot to say.

"I know you are well acquainted with The Chronicles and of course there's plenty in there but here's the thing," and he paused for maximum dramatic effect, "there are sections few Spiders can properly understand, and some have never even been read."

Barry interrupted, "Excuse me, but I've been through The Chronicles from cover to cover. I admit there are passages I may not have fully understood, but at least I've read them."

"No, you're not recognising my point," said Derek. "You've seen all the words you were allowed to see and understood what you were allowed to understand but there are some teachings The Chronicles have so far kept to themselves; we call these "The Missing". Well, sometimes certain Spiders are born who are unlike every other Spider there ever was, and I'm one of them – a "Super Secret". There are not so many of us but we know from birth that there are words, phrases, sentences, paragraphs and even perhaps pages in The Chronicles never before revealed, not ever, not to anyone. Just think about it for a moment. Then, suddenly some text from The Missing is shown to one of us Supers. It only happens when the time is right for it to be seen. That's known as a "Revelation". You can imagine how I felt when it happened to me and I was given some new wisdom and a possibility never seen before throughout the centuries."

Derek smiled wistfully at the memory before continuing, "Unfortunately my Revelation was complicated because, in order for me to fully understand what I was being shown, I needed to cross-reference it with other passages already in The Chronicles. I had to work out the links for myself. Several times I thought I'd done it, but in my case the 'Underlining' has never disappeared."

"Underlining?" repeated Barry.

"Oh yes, I should explain about that too. A Super knows if they are the one chosen to receive a Revelation because every word revealed for the first time is underlined and the only place it's shown is in their copy of The Chronicles. When the Underlining disappears it means copies of The Chronicles everywhere have updated with it, because the Super has understood the teaching revealed. It can then be generally applied because when one Super understands something, we all do. Up until then the Revelation stays with the single Super concerned and remains underlined. The beauty of it is that Supers cannot mislead other Spiders by giving them incorrect interpretations. Only what The Chronicles intend can be taught. So you see, it isn't a question of needing to know everything straight away. It's actually much better to know something only when you are able to understand it, ready to understand it and most importantly perhaps, needing to understand it. That's when The Chronicles reveal it. I know this may sound complicated but really it's very simple."

Derek paused to confirm that Barry was concentrating; of course he was. "As if that's not enough I came to fully appreciate, through my Revelation, that what is shown doesn't always make immediate sense. I had unanswered questions, complicated matters, puzzles arising. Why? I thought about it for ages before I realised there were related words and explanations The Chronicles were not prepared to show me, either because it wasn't my time or because they must firstly be revealed to another. I couldn't be shown them out of turn so I simply didn't have the answers. Now you're here I sense we will be given some sort of key to enable my Revelation to be understood and so the Underlining will disappear. The Chronicles everywhere will then update and the teaching can be taught."

"Now I'm here? Me?" stammered Barry. "What difference do I make?"

"You?" said Derek. "I think you are a Super, like me; in fact I'm certain of it. I knew it as soon as I heard the Magic Song. Clearly you are still young and nowhere near the finished article but nonetheless I can tell. Mrs Porter suspects it too; that's why you were taken to the warehouse and very nearly frozen. The Witches needed to get rid of you quickly, but we have been watching over you and so I intervened."

"We?" Barry repeated. "Who else is involved?"

"The Fairies, of course," said Derek.

"The Fairies?" quizzed Barry, his mind reeling with all this information. "Who are they? Where do they come into this?"

"They live alongside us in a hidden world and although I have never got to see them, or even spoken directly with them, there was an unexpected contact to come out of all my efforts and they sometimes send messages to me. Anyway, like I said, because I wasn't understanding all I was being shown, my Revelation remains underlined, even to this day. It's been a big regret of mine."

"What? I really don't understand this." Barry had no idea what Derek was talking about.

Derek sighed, "Listen Barry, there are many things you don't yet understand, but you will. In fact the day will come when I somehow sense you will know much more than any of us and deep down you must know it too; but that's not for now. Everything needn't be immediate. When The Chronicles initially indicated to me there was a Fairy Land alongside ours I didn't rush off to try and take advantage of all the possibilities. At the beginning I couldn't really see the point of Fairies, but then more and more things became clear and I realised that to keep the growing power of the Witches at bay we needed all the help we could get. So I began the journey to try and reach them. I had been shown how to get started because it was time to do so and that was why I'd been given the Revelation. In fact, I think amongst all the Supers, I've been given the best relationship with Fairy Land and it's up to me to make sure we keep the contact alive."

Barry was still listening with rapt attention even though it seemed thoroughly confusing, but Derek was convinced that there was much to learn from his experiences and he clearly liked talking about it all.

"The passage towards Fairy Land is a strange place in itself.

It's as if you are leaving the image you see and moving towards another you can't reach. It was like nothing else I'd ever felt; it is so very different," said Derek mysteriously. "Words can't explain some things."

"Why can't they?" asked Barry innocently, although he knew it was true.

"Well, as an example, you can consider letters and numbers. If a new letter was introduced it would make hardly any effective difference to language because we have all we need. Yet if we found a new number between one and ten the impact would be extraordinary. So what is the difference between a number and a letter? The answer cannot be properly explained in words and that's the difference."

"Surely we could…" began Barry by way of a reply.

"Don't worry too much about nitty-gritty details for now," interrupted Derek, "the main things in life are often much more straightforward. Remember, with Fairy Land you would be entering a separate different world, and I mean completely different – not just a bit. So if you ever need to go there, be prepared and keep that in mind. Now, in contrast, no Fairies can ever enter our world, although they can see into it when they wish. So they were watching and when you and the Witches were about to come together in that warehouse they told me through the contact I had established; you really shouldn't have been relying on cats you know, totally untrustworthy. Anyway, after that it was easy; I got myself along and came to your side just in time. I was able to take us both towards Fairy Land; no Witch usually wants to go in that direction. Afterwards I contacted Martin and moved us into his garden; that's where we are now. It was so nice to see him again. The Witches weren't interested in Daisy. She wasn't even in the warehouse; they wanted you. It emphasises how important you must be."

Barry tried to get up but his legs wouldn't move very well.

"That'll wear off," said Derek looking at him. "The Witches put some strong cold spells on you. There were quite a few of them there so it's only to be expected; they work better together."

Barry wasn't happy; he wasn't used to being helpless and didn't like it. Yet he realised the best thing he could do was to get his strength and powers back. He had lots to think about – he hated not understanding anything.

The next morning it was time for Derek, Martin and Barry to have another talk.

"Your arrival changes everything," said Derek. "Neither we nor the Witches can currently gain a decisive advantage, although lately they have been gathering strength. Now you're here we will see a difference; an extra Super goes a long way. Who knows how you can help and what you might yet reveal in The Chronicles?"

Barry looked at them, seeing expectation in their eyes; he certainly didn't feel worthy of it.

"Hold on. All this stuff about Super Secrets, Fairies, Underlinings and Revelations from The Chronicles is new to me. I know about The Witches from my time with Martin and I've somehow come to realise that I'm probably a Super. I can accept the responsibilities of that but I don't see myself on some sort of mission to rid the world of evil. When it comes to Witches I am really inexperienced, so much so that I told Charlie to ask you to come along and give me some advice. Did you ever get that message?" he asked turning to Martin.

Martin said, "No, I didn't and it was inexperience on your part to trust a cat. The best way to send me a message at this time of the year is on butterfly wings. Look Barry, there's no choice in all this; it's a matter of problems and solutions really. There's a problem with too few Supers and growing numbers of Witches and there must be a solution to that – and if Derek says you're part of it then you are; it's just not your time to know it yet."

Derek was growing impatient. "Look, we can't stay here. The Witches will have seen you escape from their clutches in the warehouse. They know it could only happen through a Fairy Land contact. That signifies that I was there, and with my involvement your Super status will be confirmed. I've been keeping a low profile, so something major must have brought me back into things. They may not have known that before but now they will be looking for you everywhere and will start in those places where you've been seen; this house and garden will be on their radar because of the encounter with Mrs McGaw. We've got to go."

"I can't go anywhere," said Barry. "I've got my family to consider and there's always something needing attention in the neighbourhood. I'm not running away from a bunch of Witches."

"Oh yes you are," Derek replied.

"Oh no I'm not!" said Barry.

This standoff wasn't progressing too far, but the Spiders

soon had other things on their mind because deep underground, the Witches had also been assessing events in the warehouse.

Mrs Porter was speaking.

"It was a good job I was there and could see for myself what happened. You lot were completely useless as usual but I can't blame you for it this time. I smelt Derek again, and then he and that little Spider disappeared together; it tells me something. I last saw him here in our Great Hall years ago. We thought we had him but he escaped through some sort of vanishing act after spinning that awkward heat spell on us. I don't know yet exactly how it happens but he can definitely go outside our reach. He's been keeping quiet for a while but something has brought him back and it's clearly the new Spider! If that's two Supers co-operating then we've got a big problem with their combined powers working against us."

All the Witches were watching her nervously; none of them spoke.

"So let's see. If they disappeared together it's a fair bet to assume they're together now – but where? I want them found. That little one – Barry – he's the one to concentrate on, so I want you to visit everywhere he's ever been seen; in particular, keep watching his family home. All Spiders have a great loyalty to the area where they live and he won't wish to be away from it for long. Get out, start looking and find him."

As the Witches trooped out Mrs Porter said to one of them, "No, not you."

Mrs Pugh turned around very nervously. Did Mrs Porter know about Louvain Terrace?

"Yes, Chief," she said.

"Do you recall me saying that nothing stays hidden from me for long?" asked Mrs Porter.

"Of course, many times," replied Mrs Pugh with dismay.

Mrs Porter was smiling one of her thin unpleasant smiles. "So did you think I didn't sense where Barry was living and that you'd been there recently and were planning to go again? I sent you all looking for him before just so I could see if you were trustworthy; I always knew where he was!" She paused before continuing, "What do you think I've found out about you?"

"I'm sorry, I don't know," answered Mrs Pugh, more nervous than ever.

"Only exactly what I thought, that you are not to be trusted, just like our cat friends. Perhaps that's why cats and Witches get along so well, eh? I'd seen Barry trying to gain their help through Charlie, but it's easy to make cats a better offer. I told them to follow those children to school and then send a report back saying the young one was in great danger; Barry soon came hurrying to the scene. However, the really important thing is what happened next, a Super appeared at his side and they both disappeared!"

She continued, "That tells me a lot of things well above your level of knowledge, but you could at least have said why you thought a Secret was in Louvain Terrace. There was no need to say you were certain of anything. You had the chance to give me information but didn't. So now you must take this punishment potion. For the single reason you told me no lies I have been kind. I'm not sure but perhaps you may even have meant well;

nonetheless, I need the absolute trust of those around me, so you are henceforth removed from our sisterhood of Witches and condemned to lead a very unhappy life with Mr Pugh living as people. All your time as a Witch will be erased completely from your mind."

Mrs Pugh drank the potion and does not feature again in these pages except as a memory.

Left alone, Mrs Porter picked up her copy of the *Witches Reference Book*. The chapter she wanted to read was headed, "Super Secrets and How to Handle Them". She had a plan.

Back in the garden the sun had gone underground and the three Spiders were making a move.

"This way," said Martin. Derek and Barry followed him down a well-worn path into the smallest of openings within a wall.

"This won't do. Here we are, hiding away like common criminals," said Barry. "It's embarrassing; what will everyone think of me?"

"You still have much to learn," said Derek. "Where there is a greater need, then there is a greater purpose – that's what The Chronicles make clear. Remember?"

"Yes but…" Barry wanted to argue but couldn't speak to contradict The Chronicles. His voice just trailed away.

In any case, Mrs McGaw was approaching as if she knew exactly where they were. She was sniffing the air again and again. It hadn't taken long to track down the Spiders.

"They smell us," said Derek.

"That's easily fixed – just watch," said Barry.

As Mrs McGaw came closer, still sniffing, she suddenly began to sneeze. She sneezed and sneezed and sneezed, she couldn't stop. Her eyes started watering too; nothing else was on her mind.

The Spiders walked straight past her; she didn't care.

"Very good," Derek commented. "Not sure I know that one."

Barry grinned at him, "I've used something similar before with coughs."

Derek looked puzzled but impressed.

"Never mind the admiration society," said Martin. "Look ahead, another Witch."

In front of them stood Mrs Crier! They knew she had heard the sneezing and could plainly see them. They all looked at each other for a few seconds and then she called out to the other Witches nearby.

"Here they are, over here, this way." She quickly moved in the opposite direction, pointing in front of her. Shapes appeared from everywhere following her away from the Spiders.

A quick web-thread journey and they were safely hidden in the garden shed, back at Barry's family home, with time to consider what had happened.

"That was unbelievable," said Martin. "Derek, can you explain why a Witch would help us escape?'

"I could," he answered, "but not now."

Naturally Barry wasn't satisfied with that, but before he could say anything Sinbad appeared.

"What's going on?" he asked Barry. "Who are these?" indicating Martin and Derek.

"Ah, just a couple of my friends. I was showing them round. We'll be gone soon," he replied.

Sinbad looked them up and down, his eyes seeming to dwell on Derek for a moment.

"No problem," he said and added, "let me know if there's anything I can do to help," before walking off towards some bags of compost stacked in a corner.

"What I don't understand," said Barry to Derek, "is why we headed back towards Louvain Terrace? It's obvious the Witches will soon be here looking for me."

"You'll see," said Derek. "It's sometimes important when dealing with your enemies to do the expected. It's late now, let's see what happens tomorrow."

The next morning when Martin and Barry woke up, Derek was gone.

"There's no point looking for him," said Martin. "If Derek doesn't want to be found then you won't find him, it's as simple as that."

"I still can't understand why he brought us back here," said Barry.

A giant ant suddenly appeared. "My name is Spanner; we're ready," he said.

"Ah, good … ready for what?" Martin inquired.
"The next stage, of course," said Spanner. "That's the message I've been told to give you; we're ready," and off he went as quickly as he came.

"That's welcome news, I suppose, but a little late," thought

Barry to himself remembering how he had been tricked by the cats. At the moment he didn't know what the next stage would be; things had moved on. It was no longer a simple matter of keeping an eye on Daisy.

He turned to Martin, "Don't worry about that. It's not important for now. What's happening with Derek?"

"I'm sure we'll find out soon," Martin said. "In the meantime my job is to look after you."

"I don't need looking after," Barry indignantly replied.

"That's what the young always say. Listen Barry, you may not know this yet, but if you really are a Super who can help us find hidden passages in The Chronicles, then who knows what you will be able to add to our knowledge? That's really important, and when you're my responsibility then nothing, and I mean nothing, is going to harm you."

Barry could see that Martin meant every word and so there would be no point in arguing. Instead he wondered some more about the ants. How could he put them to good use in the new circumstances?

Derek had been right to suspect that Mrs Porter could tell Barry was no ordinary Spider. Her plan to fix him, and all the Supers once and for all, started with Charlie.

Witches and cats had many things in common but the main thing was that they cared for themselves and nothing much else. There was never a thought of doing good just for the sake of it or because someone asked you; in short they did very little without an underlying reason of self-interest. This shared approach helped Witches and cats understand each other.

Probably few people ever think about how many cats live away from family homes but the numbers are too numerous to count. You can be sure they cover a large area and will be living completely different lives from those cats you do know about. The Witches knew it was only a matter of giving them a selfish enough purpose and many things could be achieved.

Yet Charlie was a bit different from most other cats; he had a rare intuition that few other felines possessed, but even that did absolutely nothing to reduce his selfishness. Therefore, although sometimes willing to carry urgent messages, he could never be totally trusted.

Because of their unreliability Barry had at one time even thought about asking Tombstone, the family dog next door, to help him but it was completely hopeless. Tombstone only wanted to jump around and bark a lot and Barry soon realised cats have talents that dogs do not. Yet the problem of their unreliability remained and Mrs Porter knew it.

So, perhaps this is a good point to remind you where we are in my telling of Barry's adventures. After living quietly at home with his people-family he met a Secret Spider called Martin, and had his first encounter with the Witches. This led him to a Super Secret called Derek who thought Barry was actually also a Super Secret. Derek explained there were parts of The Chronicles that had never been seen, they were called The Missing. When one of these became visible it was called a Revelation.

These were only initially given to a Super and remained underlined until understood, then the underlining disappeared. The Witches, led by Mrs Porter, needed to stop Barry at all costs before his powers fully developed to the stage where he might also be given new and important Revelations. She knew that ultimately these could result in the Witches being defeated in their plans to capture the minds of selected little children.

8.

The Missing

Barry had been reading The Chronicles. He often glanced through them, but from time to time he felt he should read them much more carefully, and now it led to him wearing a deeply puzzled frown. Usually he understood everything he was reading, even to the point where he felt as if he might have written it himself. Yet on this particular day he was struck by a paragraph in the "Misuse of Power" chapter. It seemed to be something he'd not noticed before and so wondered about Revelations, Supers and The Missing for a moment, but the wording itself was soon of greater interest to him.

"Spiders must remember why it is much easier to be a success when you have already been successful, but nothing succeeds like trying to achieve greater goals. This requires an understanding that all true authority and influence should be both gained and temporary and how every objective must be reset."

What did it mean? he wondered. Why had it never struck him before? The whole thing was a mystery, but Barry at least reasoned it couldn't mean he was somehow receiving a Revelation by mistake, because the text wasn't underlined. Still, when he looked again the new paragraph, Number 68 in Chapter 2, was on the page before him in plain black and white.

Yet, as is the way with Secrets, another entirely different matter soon landed itself at Barry's door: fresh elections to the Surgery Parliament. So for the moment he put aside the complexities of The Chronicles and concentrated on matters closer to home.

You will recall that Barry had been chosen to represent the views of his neighbourhood at local meetings; he enjoyed the responsibility and wanted it to continue. He always liked to help everyone, be useful and spread kindness when possible. The role was also an opportunity to meet a variety of creatures and learn more about their lives. Barry had been elected to the post because of a certain air of knowledge and confidence he possessed; it could be seen by all Spiders. However, there are no jobs for life and Spider society has a system whereby the position of officials is regularly reviewed. That was happening to Barry; it was time for the next election.

The complication was that in the attic of Barry's family house lived a Spider called Lawrence who was also a candidate. The rumour was that he had a lot of supporters in the upper half of the house whereas Barry was favoured on the ground floor and in the garden. Barry had never even met Lawrence but it was clear he felt a degree of rivalry.

"He's not getting my job!" Barry told Sinbad. "There's too much to do for one thing, what with the ants creeping closer and closer and the general need to improve garden life. Then there's that rumour about the family's wish to redecorate – painting always causes lots of disruption and upset; we need to keep our eye on that! This Lawrence has no experience or track record of community service; he never even comes down this way. Frankly, he's an unknown quantity and I'm sure I can do better for everyone."

Sinbad did not need convincing. "I totally agree. We can't have a Larry in the job just after a Barry! It's too confusing, our area will be a laughing stock but on a serious note, you're right. We don't know anything about him and he can't expect to be elected when we understand nothing about his policies or his relationship with the people-family. I was your election manager last time and I'd be proud to do it again. I think you do a good job and I'm not the only one. You've got everybody's trust and that's something hard to find amongst our lot. I don't want some upstairs Spider representing me. They have a different way of looking at things from there and even more so when they come from the dark attic – those Spiders really can't tell the wood from the trees."

They both laughed; it was agreed.

That night Barry was cleaning around his little house and, as always, thinking hard, although it was difficult to tell exactly what went on in Barry's mind at any particular time. Apart from all his Secret thoughts and the problem of the Witches, and discovering more and more powers with the accompanying insights they bring, there was the wellbeing of his people-family to consider. He was also studying The Chronicles, trying to learn what they explained, together with general local community matters where there was always tension just under the surface between Spiders, ants and other creatures. Finally, there was now the current local election.

Suddenly, out of the darkness, Barry heard a voice saying, "Anybody there?"

Who would ask a question like that? Everyone downstairs knew Barry and where he lived; turning around he saw another Spider.

"Hello, Jeffrey," said Barry. "We don't often see any of you upstairs Spiders down here in the kitchen. What brings you visiting?"

Jeffrey didn't immediately reply because, as is the way with Spiders, they sometimes spend time just being where they happen to be. It then becomes easier for them to understand exactly what they have to do and deal with.

"Don't stand for re-election," Jeffrey said after a moment.

Barry looked at him intently. "Why not?" he asked.

Jeffrey walked around, looking at where Barry lived. "I've never actually been in this part of the kitchen before, have I? We've met a few times around the house and I keep hearing lots about you but I've never been in here; very nice and so handy." He looked straight ahead without making any eye contact and added, "I've agreed to be the election manager for Lawrence. I don't think you've met him?"

Barry shook his head, saying nothing.

"No, I wouldn't have thought so," continued Jeffrey, glancing upwards. "He lives in the attic, not even upstairs, and has always kept away from everybody. I only got to know him when there was a leak in the roof a few months back but he's not a bad sort."

Barry stayed quiet.

"In fact when we got talking I realised how we could all get a benefit from bringing him more into the life of the house; you know, stop him being such a recluse. I came to see that he had a good deal of common sense and wanted the best for everyone. Now, of course I realise he's not in your league," he looked inquiringly at Barry, but there was no reaction so he kept going. "I'm older and have seen and heard many contrary things and there's one thing I clearly sense, you are a Spider that must concentrate at a higher level than local politics. Lawrence will look after things around here on behalf of everybody because you're needed elsewhere."

After that somewhat awkward beginning they talked long into the night. It even got to the stage where Barry brought up the subject of Chapter 2 paragraph 68, and what Jeffrey said about it gave him even more to consider. By early morning he had agreed not to stand at the local election.

The next day Barry saw two of the shed Spiders during his afternoon patrol.

"We're all set," said Sinbad. "Lawrence doesn't stand a chance."

"Dead right. Spiders from upstairs don't think like us or see the world like we do. There's more of us than them anyway so the election's in the bag," agreed Splash.

Sinbad said, "I've spoken to lots of garden Spiders about it and there's nobody who wants an attic Spider representing their interests. It's never happened before and we all like the way things are right now – nothing is going to change." With those remarks, said with a great deal of emphasis, Sinbad and Splash left to go about their business.

Barry knew this was another problem for him to solve.

"How do I not stand for office without upsetting everyone?" he thought. "Even more than that, how can I get Spiders to vote for someone they've never met, only dimly heard of and certainly don't trust as their local representative?"

There was only one way Barry could see; it was by using The Chronicles. The new paragraph he'd noticed fitted the bill exactly. He set about putting the wheels in motion by visiting Derek.

All Spiders knew Derek was a highly regarded Super, even though no one except Barry knew that he had once been given a Revelation. Don't forget that the Underlining was still visible and so other copies of The Chronicles had never updated. You might also note again that the Super granted a Revelation is not identified.

Derek had gained quite a reputation. Youngsters were told tales of his deeds and whatever he said carried a good deal of weight because a Super has a sort of guidance or interpretative role in Spider Land. This doesn't mean there are new teachings arising every five minutes for Supers to unravel. Most sections of The Chronicles are straightforward and understandable to all Spiders, and of course any published passage can't be changed. It's just that every so often some new text from The Missing is revealed and needs to be considered. Over many centuries some legendary Super Spiders have been shown some of these but others remain unseen, waiting their time and turn to be revealed. Derek was thought to be one of the Supers best able to explain what The

Chronicles intended.

Barry took off by web-thread to find him.

Derek had been trying to keep a low profile because he knew he was being hunted by Mrs Porter and her Witches. Nevertheless, without hesitation he came out of hiding when he sensed Barry wanted to see him. They agreed to meet at his hidden house near a thick forest where people never visited.

"I'd like you to come and speak in our family garden to my lot and explain more about something I was reading in The Chronicles. It's the section where it talks about "the greater goals". I think it can be spun to mean that Spiders should not be re-elected for office in consecutive periods because it would be a bad thing for democracy. That's the best reason to give why I can't stand again for local representation and you will know, more than anyone, that we have other things to do."

Barry had decided to assume Derek would know exactly what he was talking about, but stared at him with keen interest to judge his reaction.

"What are you saying?" said Derek looking puzzled. "There's nowhere in The Chronicles that mentions greater goals in that way."

"Yes, there is! It's in Chapter 2 where it says how it's important to spread any degree of authority as widely and as often as possible, how it should be gained but temporary and so on." Barry was now looking equally puzzled. "Don't you know it?"

Derek needed some time to collect his thoughts. After what seemed an age he said,

"I've told you The Chronicles have hidden parts and that from time to time they are revealed to certain Super Secrets; these parts are known as The Missing. Supers have received them over the years as Revelations and I myself had the good fortune to have an entire missing paragraph revealed to me a while back when it needed to be known. Now you come here to tell me something like this?"

It was clear that Derek had deep misgivings about Barry's comments and he walked purposefully over to fetch his own copy of The Chronicles. Derek didn't often read it these days, unless of course his senses told him a new Revelation had become available. All new teachings were always of the greatest possible importance and interest, but he'd had no indication of that happening. He picked the book up and brought it over.

"So, show me," he said.

Barry turned to the "Misuse of Power" chapter where paragraph after paragraph was displayed, all neatly numbered and following on, one after another.

"It's right there, paragraph 68 out of 115 paragraphs," and Barry read out the passage I quoted earlier; he looked again at Derek.

"You must have this wrong, Barry. There are only 114 paragraphs in the "Misuse of Power" chapter, and that's been the case for many years," said Derek.

"Well, look for yourself; it's there for all to see," Barry said, passing the book to him in frustration because there seemed no room for argument on what was plainly visible.

Derek stared at the page and there they were, 115 paragraphs in Chapter 2, with a paragraph 68 he hadn't seen before.

"Was this paragraph underlined?" he asked Barry after a few moments.

"Of course not. I did wonder about that after all the stuff you were telling me; Revelations, Missings, Supers and whatever but it wasn't underlined so it can't be anything special," answered Barry, sounding as if he wanted confirmation of the point. "I thought it must just be a few lines that somehow I hadn't noticed."

"No, Barry, you can't notice what isn't available. Listen, I haven't told you quite everything," Derek said with his voice quivering. "Supers also know there are important missing paragraphs that will not be revealed to any of us. They stay hidden and will remain so until the time is right for a very special Spider to see them."

He was speaking in a whisper, "The paragraph you have shown me is definitely part of The Missing and so it's a new teaching in The Chronicles that no one else has ever seen. Yet you say it wasn't underlined and so…" his voice trailed away as if he was lost in thought. It seemed to be a big moment.

He looked again, studying every word in paragraph 68 very hard indeed.

"Barry, I think you must be the Supreme Secret Spider we've been waiting for."

Everything stayed quiet as Barry and Derek stared at each other.

"Stop talking such rubbish," Barry spoke eventually breaking the silence. "I know I'm a Secret, fair enough, but I'm still not totally sure about being a Super and if anything this proves I'm not, because the paragraph wasn't underlined. To talk of me being the Supreme is madness."

However, he sounded a little more unsure. Barry had shown Derek something in The Chronicles that had been confirmed as part of The Missing; it did take some explaining because things of that nature were clearly few and far between. There could be no dispute that there were now 115 paragraphs displayed in "Misuse of Power", with a new paragraph 68.

"Listen to me, Barry. This is not just a missing paragraph," said Derek. "Don't you see? It wasn't underlined, yet you were able to show it me, in my own copy of The Chronicles. I couldn't see that teaching until then but now all Spider copies throughout the world will have updated. The point I'm making is that the Revelation was only visible to you until it was instructed otherwise **by you**, whether understood or not."

"Then there's this," he said pointing underneath paragraph 115. "A line has appeared telling me that Chapter 2 is now complete. These so-called "Draw" lines are never shown to Secrets or below and Supers don't talk of them to others. You don't see a line at the end of the chapter do you?"

Barry shook his head.

"So that's more evidence. This particular Draw line is foretold to happen as one of the means to tell Supers that the Supreme Spider is at last in the world; the final missing paragraph in this particular chapter shall be revealed only by him. No Draw lines are visible to you simply because nothing can be closed or complete to the Supreme. There is another sign but believe me those first two are enough for now."

"I still don't think it's anything to do with me," said Barry.

"You are stubborn, aren't you?" interrupted Derek. "Listen, you get to know what you need to know when you need to know it, remember? Right now, there's no doubt at all in my mind, you are without question the Supreme; you just don't believe it yet. What obviously happened was that you were born as a Secret, like Martin. Then at some point you grew directly into being the Supreme, and you still need to adjust to the change."

Derek still had much to say, "Perhaps I should have realised before but I thought you were just being a bit reluctant to acknowledge yourself as a Super. That's understandable and does happen, but I could tell you were more than a Secret although I never thought this. The Chronicles must have wanted you to have an early period where you could learn about the life of ordinary Spiders; maybe even knowing people better through living with a family. There will be a purpose behind that because those of us who are high ranking don't generally live near people or other Spiders. Anyway, as far as you are concerned, when The Chronicles wished it, and with those understandings in place, you became the Supreme; you were not born into the role but it was your destiny. The position can only be occupied when the time is right and that time is now! That's why, and when, paragraph 68 was revealed to you and why you showed it me."

Barry listened carefully as he always did, but wasn't convinced.

The next day Derek visited Barry's family home and garden and accompanied Lawrence and Jeffrey as they toured around, meeting everyone, listening and explaining their thoughts for the future. There was some disquiet about electing an attic Spider but The Chronicles had amended with 115 paragraphs in "Misuse of Power" and the Spiders could see for themselves that Barry could not remain in post. At a local representative level, and with Barry's endorsement, Lawrence was elected unopposed.

Normal Spiders had no need to know but, because of the latest Revelation, Supers everywhere were already taking action. Their senses told them the Supreme was in London and they knew that on them rested "a special duty". They had been given the sign summoning them together, and around the world web-threads were in motion; the Supers were on their way.

"Don't worry," Barry had said to the locals, "I will still be around." He was changing into all he was meant to be because it was a requirement of The Chronicles. Yet he had no intention of neglecting the welfare of his people-family. Whatever the future held for him he had lived life as an ordinary Spider and those roots would make him better and keep him humble.

Meanwhile events were gathering speed and destiny was approaching; it was a moment to prepare, even if Barry couldn't help but have a few lingering doubts.

"Mind you," he thought to himself, "funny how Jeffrey told me that the answer to my question would be found with Derek, and The Chronicles did show me a missing paragraph just when it was needed. Then there's that business about Draw lines, and it's true that I still don't see any. I'd developed a suspicion I was more than a Secret; that in itself is pretty amazing, and I do seem to be getting a lot more powers and insights by the hour. Yet am I really the Supreme Spider who has been talked about for generations? It seems too unlikely."

Later I shall need to explain more about how and why the Witches received reactions to Revelations, but for the moment it's enough to say that, in consequence to what she had been reading, Mrs Porter was also thinking very hard indeed.

Revelations

"There's been a Revelation!" It was the only thing being talked about.

You must always remember that when there is a Revelation from The Chronicles nobody knows where, when or to whom it was given. It could have been to any Super, at anytime and anywhere in the world. Copies of The Chronicles may update in due course but as to the surrounding circumstances, nothing.

However, if the truth isn't clear, then rumours begin.

I have already explained that about one in a 1,000,001 Spiders are Secrets but the numbers change dramatically to one in a 1,000,000,001 when talking about Super Secrets. They just don't come around very often.

So, as is the way of the world, an inborn curiosity arises to find out more about the Revelation, after all there are only a limited number of Supers to consider as the source. Actually, it didn't matter much to most Spiders who simply and easily adjusted to the new information and teaching; they have always been very good at that sort of thing. Other creatures were a different matter. Take ants, for example; their curiosity is overwhelming and those in Barry's garden were no exception. They had heard there had been a Revelation and when one ant knew something then every ant soon got to know, or wanted to know. Yet does that explain how within a few days, everyone was talking about Barry?

Also, don't forget that up to now, apart from Derek and Martin, no one was sure Barry was even a Secret, but suddenly there was a growing suspicion he was the Super who had been given the latest Revelation.

Of course, everything around and about Barry was being monitored as carefully as possible by Mrs Porter. She knew the Witches needed to deal with him once and for all before his powers became fully developed.

"I know who's behind this," she hissed at Mrs McGaw. "It's that little runt who helped Martin spoil our plans at Parsley Avenue. We got you into the family home and everything was moving along nicely but then the house became unbearably hot and we had to exit. I've had my suspicions about him all along, ever since I heard the Magic Song. He's something very special that one; I can sense it."

"But he's so young and little," said Mrs McGaw.

"Idiot," rasped Mrs Porter. "It's not about age or size, it's about what you are and what you may be. Didn't you ever go to Witches school in Geneva? I remember my form mistress drilling it into us over and over:

'The youthful years are yours to build upon. They shape everything you become so fill them up, fill them up, fill them up because they never come again.'

"That was what she used to say and she was right. It's why we focus on young children in our planning for power. I have to make sure Barry does not get the chance to fill up his youthful years. It would be too dangerous for us if he is allowed to become what he may be, but don't worry, I have a plan to stop him and do much, much more."

Barry was being pestered by everyone he came across with questions about The Chronicles and Super Secrets; it was intolerable.

"You'll get used to it," said Derek.

"Well, I don't want to get used to it," said Barry, "and I won't need to."

Derek looked at him quizzically, "What does that mean?"

"Nothing," Barry replied. "Don't worry about it."

The fact of the matter was that in the same way Mrs Porter could sense the great fight between good and evil, as waged by Spiders and their allies on the one side and Witches and their allies on the other, was reaching a climax, so could Barry. He didn't know what was yet to happen but did know that an ending was near.

That morning he had woken up with a new strength and understanding; the doubts he had held were disappearing. He was becoming what he was meant to be; Mrs Porter might already be too late.

Derek was also aware that Spider Land was entering a new dimension. He and Barry had been holding long conversations because there were important things Barry needed to know.

"It's time, isn't it?" Derek asked as he entered the kitchen bright and early.

"Nearly," said Barry. "We must get everyone ready."

Super Secrets from all over the world were arriving in Louvain Terrace. They were travelling quickly because of the following brief wording contained in Chapter 15, paragraph 153.

"The Supreme Spider shall give the sign foretold to those who are chosen. Through it you are summoned in haste to help at the time of completion; for now you need know nothing more."

Barry had given the sign, even if he was unaware of doing so, and later I shall tell you more about how that happened even though it has already been shown in these pages. For the moment you need only realise that he had fully accepted his position as the Supreme Spider on whose actions everything depended.

Barry knew it, the Supers knew it and the Witches knew it.

The instruction to "those who are chosen" was nearly all that remained to be said at that point in The Chronicles because they were virtually complete. So it is important to note that an ending can be revealed before instructions on how to get there. The journey can be more important than the destination if a different way provides another outcome.

If anything, Mrs Porter had underestimated how quickly things were moving, but now I need to tell you something else. Unlike Barry with the Spiders, she was not the ultimate power behind The Witches. That rested in Luciana Adela de Sanchez, commonly called Lucy; she was the Global Chief or Head Queen Witch (known universally as the GCHQ).

From her home in central Madrid she received constant communications from Witches everywhere under a system as old as the hills and much better than the best of modern technology. For many centuries Witches had fought Spiders and were always watchful for signs that the Supreme had arrived somewhere on earth to complete The Chronicles. The importance of this was that Witches knew The Missing included information to defeat them completely, never to be seen again in this world, but it would only be revealed to the Supreme. Lucy already recognised much about Barry and the potential he carried.

At garden level there were still a lot of question marks about what was happening. Amid all the rumours, Barry had stopped his daily patrols and was generally spending his time thinking about and rereading The Chronicles, but he was not alone. Derek never left his side and gradually more and more Supers were arriving.

"They can't all stay here," Barry said. "Mother will have a fit. They'll need to spread themselves around, outside in the gardens, perhaps."

"What about the ants?" said Derek. "They won't like that, and it **will be** suspicious anyway because it's obvious these aren't normal Spiders!"

"True," Barry had to agree, looking at a rather strange individual just arrived from Sweden. "I shall need to speak with them. They've always been perfectly friendly to me."

"You're not going anywhere alone," replied Derek. "I don't

trust ants. I'm not saying they're as bad as cats but still, we can't trust anything or anybody except ourselves."

Sinbad, Splash and Frankie were lazing around by the garden shed in one of their favourite spots as Barry began his search for a suitable ant to whom he could give an update on developments.

"What's going on, Barry?" asked Sinbad. "Who are these weirdos?" He pointed towards a group of Supers talking near the compost heap.

Barry paused, he felt he should say something. "Look, it's a long story but you know how we Spiders have a special place in the world because we are made happy, useful and content. Well, in return for that, a set of responsibilities **are** placed on some of us. They involve making sure as best we can that no harm comes to the innocent or the unaware. Great danger is nearby and for Spiders like me it's time to face it and stop it."

Without any hesitation, and as one, the three friends said they understood and asked if they could help; they'd known for a while that Barry was no ordinary Spider. He was quite moved by the whole thing.

Walking further into the garden he said as much to Derek. "There was I thinking it would all be a bit above the wisdom of ordinary Spiders to grasp but straight away they realised and were willing to get involved. It really is something very special to be a Spider and I'm not going to let anyone forget it from now on."

When he saw a few ants he gave them much the same short speech he'd just given Sinbad and the others by way of a background explanation. However, ants are not Spiders.

"What do you mean, Spiders are special?" "What responsibilities?" "How?" "What about this and what about that?" "We said we were ready for the next stage but what is it, has it begun?" The questions went on and on and soon Barry had had enough. If a Spider has any fault, it's probably a lack of patience in some things.

"That's too many questions from you," he said, "I came to explain why there are strangers in the garden. The full story will take too long, so for now you should simply respect the fact that they are all here trying to do good and certainly will cause you no harm if you leave them alone. However, should you be the cause of any trouble, then there'll be me to deal with." He looked at them to communicate a warning they had never felt before, then turned and went back to the kitchen.

Meanwhile all the Witches had been told to gather underground.

"Lucy's coming here," Mrs Porter announced to everyone. "What does that tell you?"

"She wants a holiday?" said Mrs Crier, trying to be funny.

Mrs Porter dispensed her most withering stare. "Idiot! This is no laughing matter. If Lucy is leaving Madrid then the Supreme Spider must be near and I think it's that little runt, Barry."

She continued, "Listen Witches, London is our town and if anyone is going to sort Barry out, it's going to be us! We don't need help from others and if we act quickly it can all be done in the next few hours. I have a plan to fix Barry, and all those Supers I sense arriving, once and for all. The first stage is already under way."

She gave an evil smile of the sort you never ever want to see, and explained to the Witches what they would need to do.

Martin was as impressed as anyone to learn there'd been a Revelation, and had heard that Supers were on the move and heading to London. He thought he should at least go and see Barry, but found it impossible to get past the security measures now in place around Louvain Terrace.

"You can't come in here." It was a Super who, as far as Martin could tell from the accent, was American. Martin felt helpless and frustrated because a giant protective invisible web had been formed, and he was on the outside trying to get in. He knew who was at the centre of things.

Wearing his best smile he said, "You may not fully understand this but I'm a close friend of Barry. My name is Martin and I've got something very important to tell him."

That didn't seem to get him anywhere.

Martin realised that desperate times called for desperate measures. "Tell him it's about Daisy; she's in danger," he added. He paused and wondered why he'd said it, he hadn't meant to.

The American Super looked Martin up and down.

"Wait here," he said, and disappeared along the path.

The nerve centre of the operation around Barry was being conducted from the new, bigger garden shed; Barry had insisted all the Supers were to be kept out of the house where possible. Inside there was a great deal of activity to the extent that the Spiders normally resident had been moved outside. Emery wasn't happy but Spider sense meant he had to go along with it. He was sitting by the door as the American Super approached.

"Out of my way, please," said the Super, who then paused. "Oh, actually you're a resident here, not one of us newcomers, eh? Could you take a message to Barry? You must know him well. I've got to get back on guard duty at the gate. Tell him there's a Spider called Martin there," and the Super relayed what he had been told to say.

Emery set off at once and soon Barry appeared. He couldn't ignore anything to do with Daisy.

"Barry," said Martin. "What's going on?"

Barry wasn't alone. Derek and some Supers were with him.

"Hello, Derek," Martin continued, "I didn't expect to see you here, who are all these others?"

"What about Daisy?" said Barry. "You said she's in danger." In the circumstances he had no inclination for small talk.

"I don't know. I have no idea why I mentioned her; it just came into my head," Martin admitted.

Barry looked displeased and thought for a moment, "Then you'd better come with me," he said, and they all went back down the path and into the shed.

Underground, the Witches were still discussing the plan Mrs Porter had devised; none of them would have had the nerve to say it was anything but brilliant.

"It's really very clever," Mrs Crier had said, "but can it possibly work?"

"You are all idiots, you really are," said Mrs Porter. "Do you think for one minute that I've reached my position of power without knowing more things than you can even dream about?

Normally I let you all deal in childlike potions, because to get into the minds of little ones they are usually all we need, but be under no illusions. I have many plans and other potions and I know the spells associated with each of them. This one is very special, of course it will work."

I should perhaps mention that most people would have the idea that if a spell involved any sort of potion, then to be effective it would need to be swallowed, but not so. Witches have developed a range of spells to take effect in different circumstances. For instance Mrs Porter had heard of something being planned that worked simply by touching the intended target; unfortunately, it was under development and currently unreliable. Yet there were other tried and trusted spells in the *Witches Reference Book* and she knew it was a question of using the right one to deal with any particular circumstance.

Yet not every Witch could use everything available; greater scope existed within most spells, depending on the Witch concerned.

In this case, to develop a spell she had already started, Mrs Porter produced a little clay image of a particular Spider and placed it on a bed of sharp thorns; around it she sprinkled a strange white powder, invisible to all except her. It had no smell and was all that remained of the bones of things that had long since stopped walking the earth. She explained what needed to be explained and while the Witches circled around and chanted in unison, she spoke in a language only a Witch knows. Finally, when it was done, Mrs Porter reminded everyone that great care was necessary.

"Remember, by now the word will be out everywhere about the latest Revelation. Why else would Lucy leave Madrid? She used to be called the queen of in-betweens because she appeared all over the place but these days she stays in Spain whenever she can. Yet now she's moving. It's all to do with that little runt, I just know it and I'm going to finish him before things get completely out of hand," said Mrs Porter. "This is much deeper than trying to get anyone drinking a punishment potion, but I have other answers. Now, everyone leave, I've got more thinking to do."

When she was alone Mrs Porter pulled out her *Witches Reference Book*. The reaction she had been reading to the **most** recent Revelation was part of the normal rhythm of life pursuing all creatures, whereby one thing leads to, and affects, another. She studied the book closely, beginning again with the section covering the meaning of Revelations and the Spiders to whom they are given. Then she read and reread the latest recommendation. Of course she didn't know what the Revelation **itself** had actually said but she thought long and hard about the possible implications for Witches.

"I bet that Revelation was given to Barry," she muttered; her senses told her so.

In the garden shed it had suddenly gone quiet.

"You're joking," said Martin after a moment of silence.

Hearing about the events of the past few days had shocked him to the core. "You're telling me that you were given the new Revelation? You? Barry?"

"That's right." Barry accepted this would be surprising news for anybody. Indeed he hadn't completely got used to it himself, although with every passing minute his mind was adjusting to the reality. He could feel change taking place, but he answered Martin with great understanding because they had been good Secret neighbours. In his new role Barry could have no friends, it is the accompaniment to great power and responsibility.

"That makes you a Super?" Martin said in a voice sounding halfway between a question and a statement. "That's unbelievable, but why all this?" he asked, pointing to the Supers in the shed.

Barry didn't answer; he was still thinking about what Martin had said at the gate.

However, Derek couldn't keep quiet for long. "Look Martin, I'm sorry but we've got to get on; there's a lot to do." He felt he had to try and maintain some perspective and urgency on things.

Barry certainly didn't have time to waste on routine questions. It was important to look ahead, but he was still concerned about Martin who clearly needed a few moments to get into his head everything that was happening. It didn't seem appropriate to reveal that Barry was actually the Supreme.

"You look a bit pale to me, Martin. How are you feeling?" asked Barry, making clear he was the one setting the timetable.

"Not so good right now, actually," answered Martin. "I suppose this news is proving quite a shock to my system."

Barry was beginning to have many new understandings flooding into his body and brain and he looked worried.

"When did it start?" he asked.

"Not long ago. It seems to be getting worse, but I'll be fine,"

Martin answered.

Barry stared at him, "Come and see me in an hour," he said. Little did anyone know as they watched Martin leave the shed that an hour would be too long.

The spell Mrs Porter had started was clearly taking greater effect as she and her leading Witches gathered together in her apartment, not far from the Great Hall. To the uninformed they were watching television, but the pictures they could see were not available on any normal channel.

The Spiders weren't the only ones who could be sent messages.

10.
New Arrivals

Two things happened at about the same time that Martin was leaving the garden shed: Lucy was on television and a parcel was delivered to 14 Louvain Terrace.

Lucy was introducing herself to everyone and laying down the law.

"Listen carefully, London Witches," she said. "Probably you know of me, but there are many more things unknown. I have been the GCHQ for nearly 200 years and I can assure you that I know everything necessary – everything! It was foretold this position would be mine and you should all keep that in mind. These are not ordinary times and so it may not be the time for ordinary actions. Something else has happened that was also foretold. The Spider you call "a little runt" (and Mrs Porter grimaced as if Lucy was talking directly to her) is much, much more than that. Do not think you can deal with him by yourselves. I will be there shortly. Wait for me."

The Witches stared intently at Lucy on screen. They saw a tall, elegant, ageless lady dressed completely in black with long red finger nails surrounded by cats of all different types, sizes and colours. Her hair was as black as the clothing she wore.

"One more thing," she added. "I have sent a parcel. It is not for you but when it arrives in London it will have some effect and begin to prepare for what must be." With that the screen went blank and Lucy was gone.

"Who does she think she is?" Mrs Porter thought indignantly. Lucy had said she knew everything and certainly seemed to have a very high opinion of Barry. A good deal of prudence looked like a sensible approach for the moment and Mrs Porter was no fool; she adopted a different public strategy.

"Lucy is the GCHQ and must be obeyed; we wait for her arrival," she said, but with no intention of doing so. This was London, she was the one in charge and her plan was already underway; the television broadcast didn't change anything.

The parcel was addressed, "Daisy Davies, London". There was no other marking but it arrived safely at 14 Louvain Terrace, all the way from Spain. The postman rang the bell, Mother answered and carried it inside.

"We don't know anyone in Spain," said Mother curiously. "Who would send Daisy a parcel from there?"

"Beats me," said Father.

Daisy wasn't bothered by all the niceties. "It's mine and I want it."

Opening the parcel seemed a perfectly natural thing to do, so they let Daisy proceed. She tore at the neatly wrapped packaging and tossed it aside; inside was the cutest little pussycat cuddly toy you have ever seen. There was an accompanying note reading in English, "My name is Rodrigo."

"Oh, he's absolutely adorable," said Daisy.

"It's all very nice of course, but who sent it?" wondered Mother.

"I don't care," answered Daisy. Yet one thing was for sure, Lucy would have had a very good reason to send Rodrigo anywhere and it wouldn't be long before that reason became clear; there was more about him to discover. You can never trust a cat, remember?

Mrs Porter was considering her options but had already realised that it would be best to involve only a very few trusted Witches in her plan to eliminate Barry and take over as the GCHQ.

She knew Lucy would soon be in London and so it seemed the right and proper time to overthrow her, but instinct told her that Barry would be much more difficult. By now she knew he was the Supreme Secret. Lucy, her own senses and the reaction received in response to the latest Revelation told her so.

Barry knew things too. He knew Daisy was in danger and that the Witches would be aware there had been an important Revelation. He also knew that he was no longer a Secret Spider, neither was he a Super Secret. No, he accepted he was the one that The Chronicles said would appear, the Supreme Secret Spider. The problem was making sense of it all. Why him? Why now? What next?

More immediately, he didn't know the details of Mrs Porter's plan, or about the imminent arrival of Lucy from Madrid, nor the fact that a cuddly toy cat called Rodrigo was in Louvain Terrace and had already stolen Daisy's heart.

Not far away, Martin felt strange but couldn't explain the feeling. How could he when the spell spun by Mrs Porter had never before been used on a Spider? Yet he did suspect that the voices and instructions he was hearing were coming from the Witches. Martin realised this was a time when anything seemed possible.

He was right. Mrs Porter had calculated that his warning about Daisy would ensure he could get close to Barry, even with the increased security now in place. The power of her spell was such that it increased in influence by the minute, and time was short. Soon Martin would have to do exactly what Mrs Porter wanted.

Rodrigo was getting to know his new surroundings. It was easy because Daisy carried him everywhere.

"What is that thing?" Jessica had remarked, pointing dismissively.

"He's mine," said Daisy clasping her new best friend even closer to her heart, "and it's not a thing, his name is Rodrigo."

"What sort of name is that?" questioned Jessica.

"It's his name," said Daisy defensively, "and you can't touch him."

"I wouldn't want to anyway, I'm grown up," and Jessica strode off purposely towards her bedroom and a laptop computer.

Mother was next to experience the new order.

"I'm not hungry," Daisy said.

"But it's your favourite," Mother replied.

"I don't care. I'm going to play with Rodrigo," Daisy answered and ran up the stairs.

Martin was starting to feel more and more helpless within the spell taking him over. He'd seen Barry no more than 40 minutes ago, and initially thought to stay in the garden before meeting him again after the hour had passed. However, he decided to spend a few minutes inside the house, and was walking down the hall away from the kitchen when Rodrigo suddenly appeared, barring his way.

"My mistress told me about you. I suppose you already know you are in great danger, but don't worry I'm here to help," said Rodrigo.

Martin sized up this newcomer, "Who are you, what's happening and who is your mistress?" he asked.

"You don't look well at all; never mind. Oh, she's somewhere not far away; don't be concerned about it. She has her own reasons for saving your life. Take this and taste it; one lick is all you will need. It will save and protect you from the spell taking you over."

Rodrigo handed over a small colourful sweet and in a flash was gone back upstairs to Daisy's room.

Martin wasn't convinced he should lick anything but what was he to do? Rodrigo had confirmed what he suspected already, that a spell was taking him over. He was feeling weaker every second with a host of unusual sensations, and they were starting to be overpowering. His mind was being told to do things he didn't want to do; they were about Barry. He couldn't bear the thought he might be forced to try and cause Barry harm, but his imagination was racing with possibilities.

In spite of his instincts there was a big temptation to lick the sweet, and he did actually put it to his mouth, but something kept making him pause. Instead he decided to hide it in a corner of the nearby broom cupboard. Then the hour was nearly over and Martin headed towards the kitchen.

Barry had ordered that his home under the sink was not to become crowded with other Spiders; only Derek was there because he mostly refused to leave Barry's side. When Martin appeared Derek became watchful; he wasn't a Super for nothing and looking at Martin he could see something was wrong.

"Stay over there, Martin. Don't come any closer. You don't look well to me. Something's happened, or is happening, to you!" he said.

"Barry, it's me! Tell Derek not to be so silly. We have to talk about Daisy, she's in danger."

"What do you mean?" Barry said. "It's the second time you've said that."

Martin looked furtively around, "We must speak in private, not here."

Mrs Porter had always wanted Barry and Martin alone in surroundings she could more fully control, and in his own new found confidence Barry was fully prepared to oblige. He was becoming more and more sure of his powers and moreover he could take no chances where Daisy was concerned. He told Derek to stay where he was and left the kitchen with Martin. They walked down the hall together to the edge of the family living room where something made Barry stop.

Mother could be seen at the far end getting ready to go shopping; the girls were in school and Father was at work.

"No, this isn't far enough, Barry. We have to go outside the protective web," pleaded Martin. "You have to leave here and…"

"Hold it right there," said Barry. "You should know that I am aware of many things. You are under the control of the Witches but Mrs Porter is no longer a threat to me or Daisy, and you are not a threat to us either. You are being told to do things and say things designed to cause me harm, but trust me when I say that the spell on you is not important. I am the Supreme Secret Spider and there is only a single Witch with the power to cause me a problem."

With that, just as Mother was leaving, the front door bell rang. Barry stiffened and immediately went on high alert.

Mother opened it. "Can I help you?" she asked.

"Yes, I believe you can, just by listening to me for a moment," answered the tall woman who stood right at the edge of the protective web. Lucy had arrived in Louvain Terrace, just as Mrs Pugh had done some time before.

Barry quickly ushered Martin back into the kitchen, "Everything is different, now it begins," he said. "I have to go, but don't lick that sweet.

He called to Derek and said, "Take care of Martin, he is no use to the Witches when he is not near me and the spell over him will count for nothing very soon. When that happens he will fully recover."

Barry desperately wanted to re-enter the sitting room near to where Mother and Lucy were talking at the door but it was impossible. The respective leaders of the Spiders and the Witches were already the closest together they'd ever been and both were very aware of the other; any closer and the forces released might be uncontrollable. Barry left the house via a small Spider opening and went down the garden path back into the shed.

Lucy sniffed the air and continued explaining something to Mother.

"You see, Daisy is at a very vulnerable age in her development and it is so important that she gets the right teaching at this time of her life. We can help. As a very ancient society our task is to ensure that the best and brightest of children are able to flourish and make a full contribution to the world order. Of course this is a very big decision for you and your husband. It would mean Daisy leaving Louvain Terrace and being placed in our school of wonder located in Geneva. All costs and fees would of course be met in full by our Foundation." She smiled her best and brightest smile, her long red fingernails glistening in the light, before giving Mother her card. Lucy turned and seemed to float down the steps and onto the pavement before departing from sight.

It is a remarkable thing that people, and parents especially, always hear what they most want to hear when it comes to their children. If all are young then all are vulnerable and Lucy was no ordinary teller of tales or maker of promises. When she spoke it could be as if she was accompanied by the most beautiful singing you have ever heard; she was impossible to resist. There was no need to threaten, instead she beguiled and that is a deadlier weapon to use on the innocent.

In any event Lucy didn't really want to take Daisy to Geneva any time soon. All she needed was to involve herself in Daisy's life, even in the remotest possible way, because that would be something Barry could not ignore. Any trap needs bait, and Daisy was the best bait possible.

Rodrigo was watching Barry depart into the garden shed surrounded by half a dozen or so Supers; he knew his mistress was at the door talking to Mother and knew what was being said. He had no part to play there; his job was elsewhere.

From a place on the bedroom windowsill he also watched Lucy leave and later saw Father, Jessica and then Daisy arrive home. She came upstairs immediately and gathered him into her arms.

"Oh Rodrigo, I've missed you so much. That silly school won't allow me to take you to lessons but I'm back now." She looked so content.

Downstairs Father was making clear that Daisy was going nowhere.

"It's ridiculous. Who was this woman, anyway?" he said, waving her card in the air. Mother admitted she had no idea.

"When she was here, it all made such sense," she replied lamely, "but now I can't imagine what I was thinking. Of course Daisy stays with us."

It all seemed easily settled and was also for now the end of the matter as far as Lucy was concerned. Her twin objectives in visiting Louvain Terrace had been achieved. One was to meet and talk with Mother; the other was to put doubt and worry into Barry's head.

Rodrigo could watch Daisy; Lucy now had to deal with Mrs Porter.

It often happens that the ability and influence of those at risk of being overthrown are underestimated. Mrs Porter had completely failed to grasp she was dealing with real, substantial hard-core power when considering either the Supreme Spider or the GCHQ. Mrs Porter was a very strong and important Witch within her own sphere but she had misled herself and overreached into a space she couldn't occupy. In simple terms she was now "out of her league".

Lucy went straight underground from Louvain Terrace to where Mrs Porter was staying and stared at her without contempt, pity or mercy.

"You fool." It was a simple statement; Mrs Porter was instantly submissive in her presence.

She continued, "Did you really think you could take my place? I clearly told you, I told all of you, that I know everything, but you heard and wouldn't listen. You preferred to think you were better than me. There was no evidence for it but you wanted it to be true and so in your mind it became true. I watched everything you did and I knew every thought you had. I gained information from Mrs Pugh long before you knew of it, and then planted confusion in your head so you couldn't understand anything unless I allowed it otherwise."

Lucy was enjoying herself. "I spoilt your plans to capture Barry in the warehouse by letting Mrs Crier tell Derek what was happening; that fool thinks he speaks with the Fairies! She gained his trust by showing him the heat spell and I allowed it to be spun right here in the Great Hall because one small inconvenience matters nothing in the great game now being played. You have no idea what it means to be the GCHQ or the power it brings. That pathetic spell you placed on Martin to hurt Barry never had any chance of success, but I made some use of it so it continues for a while. You thought nothing of me and you know nothing of Barry. Even now you cannot recognise the strength he holds."

"I'd say sorry if I thought it would do any good," said Mrs Porter humbly. Confronted by Lucy all her hopes and ambitions were gone. The desire for unearned power has caused the downfall of many creatures; it is a danger to be avoided.

"I know," said Lucy. "The only question remaining is how shall I deal with you? It is said I have no feelings and no mercy, but that's not true because I don't recognise such emotions. I cannot afford to indulge in sentiment, thus it cannot apply to me. There will be two things. The first is you shall drink this punishment potion; I shall not describe the effect it will have because that is the second thing."

Lucy placed an ugly green coloured small bottle on the table and left the room. Mrs Porter had no thoughts and made no sound as she drank the contents; she immediately vanished completely and was never seen or heard of again.

So now, in London, the scene was set for the final trial between Spiders and Witches. Each had their leader in place, recognising each other and knowing that at stake was the history and future of the world.

Barry had been speaking with Derek and sought a quiet place to think everything through. He wondered if he should try and reach the Fairies; there was still much he had to learn.

11.

The Unnumbered

New Revelations had been coming to Barry thick and fast. They had no need to be underlined because all of them remained for his eyes only until he wished it otherwise. He was the Supreme and could decide when and whether they should be generally released into all copies of The Chronicles. He was shown every Revelation, including of course all the Revelations that had been revealed but were not yet understood, like the one given to Derek. Barry saw everything.

Some Revelations were clear and straightforward but others seemed more complex and important; it would take many hours to get to grips with all the teachings being conveyed. They were being revealed because it was the time to do so. Some hadn't been disclosed for centuries and Barry felt very humble and thoughtful to think they had waited just for him; it was certainly a big responsibility to carry.

Yet, as I've mentioned, procedural changes had arisen with Barry's arrival and so perhaps I should take a moment to recap the traditional ways The Chronicles had operated. Previously, when a Revelation was given to a Super it was underlined until it was understood. That marked the moment it was reproduced in every copy of The Chronicles throughout the world, and then the Underlining disappeared. If the Revelation completed a chapter (something that had only happened on two previous occasions, with Chapters 8 and 9), a Draw line would also appear, visible only to Supers and indicating to them that everything needed on the subject was now displayed; this was the accepted way of things.

However, Barry didn't want that approach to continue. His senses told him that these latest Revelations were of a different nature and were being given at a special moment. Only he should be aware of them, at least for the time being. He decided to block all further releases.

This was a wise move because in the past with every understood Revelation the *Witches Reference Books* automatically updated showing corresponding recommendations, suggestions and reactions. It meant that when copy Chronicles received the text of a new Revelation, the Witches were informed and advised how to react to it; this maintained the established balance. Now, Barry was keeping the Witches unaware of how they should respond to the new teachings that he alone was increasingly starting to understand. The last released Revelation had happened when Barry showed paragraph 68 of Chapter 2 to Derek. You may remember it was highly important because it heralded the onset of major changes.

Lucy was highly agitated by this new approach. She recognised the importance of paragraph 68 and realised that with the arrival of the Supreme there would be fresh Revelations for Barry to see. She felt it totally unacceptable that their *Witches Reference Books* were not being given the corresponding updates when teachings were understood, as she suspected they increasingly would be.

"It's such bad form," she muttered to herself. "It's breaking the rules! He's interfering with the order of things by keeping Revelations to himself. When they are understood we should get our reaction. That's how the world works. He's being totally unfair."

Unfortunately for Lucy, there was nothing she could do about it. Barry was the Supreme when it came to The Chronicles, and after all he was simply treating Spiders and Witches in the same way. He wanted time to understand what was being revealed as a whole, not merely in parts.

Barry thought the particularly baffling "Missing" section was in Chapter 6. This was a large chapter because it concerned itself with waste and the organisation of resources, a big subject in any society.

A new Revelation, paragraph 143, said the following:

> *"The resources available are at first always unknown but they must be completely focused on a problem; if the best solution is to appear, nothing can be wasted. The bigger a problem appears then a greater level of resource is needed, else the difficulty remains. Therefore, although all problems are equal in size the resources and commitment necessary to find the solution will vary."*

What did it mean? Barry couldn't help but think to himself

that Revelations would be even more useful if they communicated in plain and simple language. Most of the text in The Chronicles had been around for centuries and was easily instructive, yet Revelations when they appeared could be extremely baffling. It made him question himself. He was the Supreme Spider but didn't always understand what was being revealed. Why should so many Revelations be complex? Why couldn't they all be crystal clear in their instruction, and why had many not been revealed sooner?

It made Barry wonder how many problems in the world could have been avoided. The concept of Revelations appearing when they were needed made good sense, but they were only initially shown to a selected Super and even now some remained underlined. At least they were usually mercifully short but nonetheless, wouldn't you think they could be clear in content and purpose?

Looking for the best approach to understanding the information he was receiving, Barry thought about the way people dealt with their issues of learning and development. He realised there were a number of similar reference systems to The Chronicles. Yet these were never updated by their creators and he found it difficult to see why words written a very long time ago stayed completely applicable. How can past teachings best adapt to apply in the changing times, needs and circumstances of the age? Why should something written many years ago govern a modern world that has evolved very differently?

The Chronicles avoided that trap, but unfortunately caused their own problems when Revelations were selectively revealed and sometimes hard to fathom. Barry was now altering the traditional procedures still further. At least he was aware enough to worry about how the changes he had instigated could be reconciled within the overall concept of The Chronicles, namely an ongoing evolution towards an understanding of the most important mystery in life itself.

He talked to Derek about it all and received some comfort. Derek took the clear view that Barry could, in effect, do what he liked when it came to The Chronicles.

"There's never been a Supreme," he said. "It's not like those other teachings where people have had their Supreme already and the words concerned were written later by others. Who knows if they're accurate? In our Spider world we have been given a way of life that has been written by no one, yet it is written. It's very different from living under rules laid down long ago that are absolutely final, with nothing being added subsequently; we are not like that. Perhaps there is a force of some kind behind all this but that's not for us to know. We can only be what we are. Even you cannot be sure The Chronicles won't evolve and be further updated over centuries to come in the way they have been updated over centuries gone by. Something is doing it. You will need to take that into account in the judgements you make because only through Revelations can we continue to believe in and apply what The Chronicles teach. When an important meaning seems complex then it's no surprise because why should it be otherwise? Have belief that when the time is right an understanding will appear."

"I'm not sure," said Barry. "When something new is revealed to me and I find it totally confusing, then I worry about what sort of Supreme Spider I can be. I might end up making the wrong rules and I just don't see it's supposed to be like that."

"No, you're not making any rules," answered Derek. "What's happening is that teachings are being revealed to you because now is the time they're needed by you, and you are here now because this is the time you're needed. It all makes perfect sense to me because I went through something similar, albeit on a much lower scale. Admittedly, I'm not clear why the latest Revelations you've received should not be released when understood, but I imagine it's because there is otherwise a problem, and that's the solution. I don't know the ins and outs of it but that's what I'd expect. You are getting Revelations because this is when you need them; not me not anyone else – you. They will all become clear as and when The Chronicles wish it."

"Well they're not moving very far forward with the clarification, that's all I can say," answered Barry, "but for the moment I shall have to leave Revelations to one side. Tell me more about what happened with the Fairies," and he listened carefully as Derek explained what he knew.

"I mentioned before that The Chronicles gave me a small understanding of Fairy Land. Well, it went beyond any single paragraph so was not just a Revelation, it was also a cross-reference and a connection between different teachings. I was allowed to partially put everything together and see something previously missed because the time was right for me to do it. I realised The Missing refers to more than new words but also extends into linking paragraphs and sections together and forming meanings that no other Spider has ever previously needed to know. Looking back, I can see it all happened because I was meant to save you in the disused warehouse and probably I'm needed to tell you this right now – who knows? Nothing is random, everything has purpose."

Barry shivered when he thought back to his encounter in the warehouse with the Witches. He recalled Mrs Porter had nearly frozen him and remembered the cold, dry, clammy feeling.

"Go on," he said.

"Well, I don't really have much more to tell; the important part is that I thought I had worked out, from some connections in the existing text and my Revelation, how Fairy Land is alongside but outside our Spider world, and that I could go there. However, I wasn't sure that was necessary and didn't even try to do so for quite a while. Then it dawned on me that if nothing happens unless it's time to happen I should of course make the effort, because it must be the right time for it. Actually, I think the Fairies were expecting me; they've probably got their own version of The Chronicles. Perhaps it's common to have some sort of guide book for reference, eh?"

"You might be right there, in one form or another across all civilisations, but I remember you saying something about magic words and leaving one image behind and entering another," said Barry.

Derek looked embarrassed. "Yes, forgive me but I didn't know you very well back then and I didn't tell you everything. I'm sure Fairy Land is very different. Unfortunately, I kind of implied that we could enter it, but we can't; well, at least I couldn't. The best I could do was to get half way into what was like a waiting room. I never got further; too junior, I suppose," and he gave a little spidery laugh. "It's where I took you once."

"I dimly remember," said Barry, "but I wasn't myself at the time. It was a very pale place as I recall with floating shapes able to pass through anything. I don't have in my mind a traditional image of a Fairy or a place where they might live; nothing like that."

"They don't live there, you were in a waiting room," Derek reminded Barry. "You can stay in it without an ability or a commitment to go any further; it's like a sanctuary. I've no idea what Fairy Land looks like or, come to that, what a Fairy looks like. There was one more strange thing that happened though. I didn't tell you or anyone else before, although I've hinted at it when talking to Martin, but I met a Witch in the waiting room and we've spoken since, a few times; it's been useful. She told me about the heat spell for instance."

"Mrs Crier," said Barry.
"How did you know that?" wondered Derek, but Barry didn't reply.

"There's not too much to go on, though," said Barry. "I wonder if The Missing are calling me to that waiting room, and perhaps beyond? Tell me how far you think you reached in cross-referencing connections and paragraphs in The Chronicles, and don't worry any more about failing to put it all together. I have seen what was revealed and you were only meant to take things so far."

"I came to hope that was the case," said Derek, "but it's a relief to be told I made no mistakes in understanding key meanings.

Barry confirmed things sympathetically. "No, it's truly not not like that. It is all much more complex. If anything you tried too hard and went beyond what was needed."

Derek and Barry spent a while talking about the cross-referencing of paragraphs and the possible interactions, but before any next steps could be taken in the direction of Fairy Land there was still the matter of Rodrigo and Daisy.

Don't forget that using Mrs Porter's spell, Lucy had caused Martin to hide a special sweet in the broom cupboard. Then she only needed to wait for Barry to intervene after Rodrigo ensured Daisy went there and picked it up. Of course Mother had taught both her children not to eat things that had been lying on the floor, but in spite of those warnings the sweet was moving closer and closer to Daisy's mouth. Then, just in time Mother walked by. Lucy knew she would and why she would.

Barry had sensed the danger and acted fast. The best solution to the problem was simple and readily available. Through the Magic Song he had formed a connection with Mother who, because the safety of Daisy was a shared concern, was suddenly and easily prompted by him to check on the wellbeing of her youngest daughter.

Mother snatched the sweet away, walked into the garden and tried to drop it into the rubbish bin, but was somehow unable to detach it from her fingers. After much shaking she eventually managed to throw it inside, "Silly, sticky thing," she exclaimed. Back underground, Lucy smiled to herself and thought again how Mrs Porter was a fool to ignore reality.

Rodrigo had been left alone for a short time, and in those moments found and spoke with Martin, but he was soon together with Daisy again. Of course he could move and talk in every language but needed to be careful to ensure no one knew such things unless it was necessary. Instead his method of communication with Daisy was through his bright blue eyes. When you looked into them it was as if you saw deep down into the sea with a feeling arising like unexpected wonder, and of course Lucy had given Rodrigo the gift of being able to plant thoughts in the minds of young children.

Naturally there was a danger in putting anything over-complicated in their heads because every boy and girl begins life with an innocent mind. It is only at a certain age that thinking can start to become vulnerable to, well, let's say "unhelpful" ideas and influences. Daisy had reached that age, but it was still early in the process and Witches had learned how best to calculate these things. In a few more months, Daisy would be ready for more but the time was not now. So Daisy looked into Rodrigo's eyes and talked to him and he explored placing certain words and thoughts into her head for the Witches to use later in their recruitment process.

Daisy was very dear to Barry and Lucy knew such a closeness could somehow be exploited in order to help the Witches in their ultimate battle against the Spiders. After much analysis of the possibilities, Lucy had decided to exploit the vulnerability by using Mother who, through the sweet, was now affected by the touching spell. It only needed to be activated.

Meanwhile, Barry had been staring hard at The Chronicles and thinking about what Derek told him with regard to cross-referencing certain words and passages within paragraphs and chapters. Yet he wasn't happy, there was still something wrong.

Derek had suggested that Chapter 3 paragraph 9 showed the start of the key interconnected parts.

"Spiders must remember how nothing will prosper by itself for itself and so, even at the beginning, nothing in itself has any real value. The world is shared by many different things but each hope and every reality is treated with equal thought and better judgement when considered together."

Then paragraph 15 within Chapter 4:

"When there is not enough, there is more. It is a question of Spiders using what has been ignored and what can be found, but as you progress and the search becomes the answer, there are choices to be made. So look again at the judgements you are making."

Next, Paragraph 29 within Chapter 5:

"Spiders are never alone. In the way we watch, then we are watched; in the way we look, then we are seen and by the way we act, so we are treated. Therefore choose wisely to avoid being judged poorly by those who have understood what cannot be taught."

Finally, Derek had sensed the key Revelation was in Chapter 14, paragraph 14:

"Everything exists or it is unreal, but to give effect to the finding, a Spider must go beyond that which is revealed and use what has been shown, for amongst many there is one alone to guide the way. If talk is merely of the things that have been done, then the time for talking is past because it has become time for the doing. All is well only when due to be so."

When Barry thought about these Revelations and the various cross-reference possibilities, he didn't feel they answered his questions. Derek had been enthusiastic on the basis of the similarities and relationship he had found in the first three paragraphs. Their different contexts were brought together in 14/14 by the phrase, "to give effect to the finding."

Barry, however, realised more than Derek was allowed to understand. It was the Supreme who was required to go beyond that revealed, using "what has been shown". He was the one looking at teachings no other Spider had ever seen and the responsibility thus rested on his shoulders. There was no reference to Spiders in 14/14; just him, "a Spider". He must surely be the "one alone".

Derek was highly regarded, and there are important connections he had identified but he was wrong in trying to take his interpretation too far. Everything can be over analysed to the point where progress becomes impossible. He did correctly cross-refer as far as paragraph 29 in Chapter 5, but should have looked no further when his search became the answer. He also failed to understand the meaning of, "what has been ignored and what can be found" and did not choose wisely thereafter.

He was, however, right that 14/14 was very important, and there will be more on this later, but it was not relevant to him and his own Revelation. That paragraph was for a single Spider, the Supreme, to understand and take forward.

For Barry, "what has been shown" involved going beyond every one of his thoughts and experiences to reach a time when "all is well". No possibility could be ignored but clearly a very major prize was assured if the right steps were taken. He wondered if the number 14 had any meaningful significance. It was a doubled reference and certainly part of the address where he lived with his people-family. Perhaps that was a mere coincidence, it might happen. Yet if nothing is ever random then it had to mean something, and so Barry then considered whether coincidence is always random. After all, living there meant he knew Daisy. These matters are indeed complex. Perhaps we should all take a moment to wonder how our own lives are shaped by choices we have made and those made elsewhere.

Barry was being shown guidance to explain how Fairies, People, Spiders, Witches and indeed every creature that was or had been, all interacted together to combine and make sense of the way life should be lived. The Chronicles had pointed Derek in a certain direction but restricted how far he could travel. Now Barry had to understand what The Chronicles were telling him to do, before perhaps trying to go further along that very same journey.

So Barry reread the latest batch of Revelations, over and over. He still felt very humble to think they had been waiting for thousands and thousands of years, just for him. Yet he had no time to dwell on the incredible because of the reality; he was in a race against time.

Another thing was that some wording now appearing was different in a way that had never happened before. In the past when a new Revelation was given it came as, or within, a numbered referenced paragraph or sequence, eventually to find a proper place in the scheme of things. The surrounding text adjusted to stay in order and the chapter completed when all was revealed.

Yet some wording Barry had received was unreferenced and therefore had no allotted place in The Chronicles. The implication was that it could fit anywhere, although surely such an approach would spoil the logical and precise way The Chronicles were otherwise written. The question then arising was whether The Chronicles could be read and interpreted in different ways, but surely that was also impossible if they were the teachings to explain how Spiders must act and interact with all other creatures.

So Barry wrestled with his thoughts. He sensed that the ultimate key to unlocking The Chronicles wasn't in 14/14; that was just an important signpost along the way. Neither was it in anything Derek had said. It was in the unreferenced passages that Barry decided to call "The Unnumbered".

There were three of these and it was true, they unlocked The Chronicles.

12.

Inside the Web

Since touching the sweet, Mother had developed a pins-and-needles type feeling in her hand; the medical books call it "paraesthesia," but in this case it was not all it seemed.

Lucy was feeling pleased with herself; she liked knowing that her plan to defeat the Spiders used Barry to make it succeed. Lucy knew about Mrs Porter's spell, and so did Barry; they both operated at a much higher level than ordinary Witches and Spiders. That was why Barry felt he had no need to be concerned about Mrs Porter, because he could leave Lucy to put a stop to her clumsy attempts at mischief. He knew that when Mrs Porter was settled, her spell would disappear and Martin would be safe. However, Lucy had preferred to take the spell over and use it for a short while to serve a specific purpose.

As the GCHQ, she was playing for high stakes in a sophisticated way. Mother was the key to the entire family, as indeed is the case with mothers in all families. Lucy therefore needed to find a way to gain influence over her without arousing the suspicion of the Spiders that Mother was being controlled. It was a requirement ruling out any direct contact until the spell could be set because by then any Spider realisation of what was happening would be too late.

This is how Lucy set about things.

To begin with, her own spell passed through the protective web operating around Louvain Terrace on the coating of a sweet, inside the parcel from Spain. That delivery couldn't be stopped because Mother had carried it over the threshold. Rodrigo then retrieved the sweet from the packaging and gave it to Martin under a pretext of concern about the spell cast on him by Mrs Porter. Under that spell, now under the control of Lucy, Martin hid the sweet in the broom cupboard. From then on, Lucy's touching spell was the only one to be progressed.

It took effect when, at Barry's prompting, Mother snatched the sweet from Daisy, something Lucy knew would happen. The spell was still undetectable by the Spiders because it remained inactive until triggered by Lucy touching the target. That hadn't happened yet but was something Mother herself would shortly cause to occur.

You might bear in mind that the sweet was always totally harmless to both Martin and Daisy. They could lick it or not, it didn't matter, and in fact nobody licked it; only contact with Mother caused it to apply. Then, after taking effect the spell could also, at Lucy's discretion, be applied to any other family member Mother touched. Mrs Porter had heard special spells like these were being developed but, unknown to her, one of them was already operative at the command of the GCHQ.

It is strange that the most important things are often taken for granted because our time is spent looking elsewhere, for example the fact that water flows downwards. It is something not perhaps so remarkable in itself, but the amount of opportunities it provides, and has provided, is truly astonishing. In the same way, we waste the opportunity to value many precious beginnings. Every single day of your life starts with the fact that you were born, yet why should something so very unlikely and remarkable be readily accepted if nothing is random? Only after a beginning can everything follow.

It is even stranger to think how people apply waste to hunger. Barry could never understand how some people eat too much food when so many in the people world are always hungry. After all, it is no bad thing to be hungry for a short time; creatures like Spiders are used to the feeling and, as long as a meal is in prospect, will think nothing of it. In contrast there are people who seemingly must eat at the very first pangs of hunger. It is much better to eat properly when necessary, not when possible.

Chapter 6 of The Chronicles discusses the subject of waste and I have already given you a very important extract to show how every problem is actually equal in size if not implication. Yet with regard to wasting time, even Spiders are guilty of failing to think in seconds; they like to progress only in hours and days, a luxury now denied Barry. He was fully engaged with The Missing but answers were needed quickly. Where were the hidden cross-references? What was the key? What about the Unnumbered? The questions kept flooding into his mind.

Mother was, of course, keeping herself busy; she always had something to do and the truth was that she liked looking after the family and the family home. It really was a hard, full-time job but, as she knew, it was the most rewarding of them all. However, even as she occupied herself with normal day-to-day business, the touching spell that Lucy had placed upon her was waiting to take effect. Through Mother, Lucy intended to reach Daisy and through her reach the ultimate goal, Barry.

Lucy knew he would be preoccupied with trying to make sense of all the information being received, plus there were the Unnumbered she didn't even know about. The current situation in Louvain Terrace affecting Mother was therefore for Martin, Derek and the other Supers to try and resolve. Lucy had calculated they would be unable to do so.

"There's something going on right here," said Derek to no one in particular. "I can sense it."

"What do you think it is?" Martin asked.

"I'm not sure. It must involve Daisy because we all know what she means to Barry. That's perhaps the only thing making him vulnerable, but we are all watching her carefully. Let's face it, there are more Super Spiders around here than have ever come together in the history of Spider Land. I'm sure a Witch can't get near her. There is also an impenetrable web protecting 14 Louvain Terrace so nothing can enter the house uninvited. So where does that leave us? Any ideas?"

"None at all," Martin replied. "In fact, I'm still totally bemused by the idea that Barry is really the Supreme. I just don't see how you can be so sure."

Derek looked slightly irritated by a suggestion from a Secret that he could be wrong about something so important, but thought he should try and explain.

"There is a third and final indication confirming the status of Barry. It was foretold that a fifty word Revelation located somewhere in The Chronicles as part of The Missing would be given to, and revealed by, the Supreme. Barry released it to everybody when he said, "It's there for all to see." You know it as Chapter 2 paragraph 68. Only Supers knew the prophecy but that Revelation means for sure that the Supreme is here and we are summoned together to gather around him. Supers are able to sense where he is and that's why they're arriving at Louvain Terrace, here in London. Barry is the Supreme, believe me; the numbers prove it. Only a single paragraph in all The Chronicles has fifty words; it was Missing and now we have it. Satisfied?"

Martin had no choice but to be convinced. He thought of the Magic Song. Perhaps he should always have realised there was more to Barry than at first appeared, yet thinking he was the Supreme Spider was not something he'd ever have considered. Anyway he accepted that was over and done; his job now was to help as much as possible until Barry returned. Luckily because he was of no further interest to Lucy, the spell on him had diluted and he was feeling much better.

Searching for answers, he thought of that cuddly looking toy cat barring his path into the kitchen, and the colourful sweet he had been holding.

"I think I know where the danger could be coming from," he said to Derek. "Leave it with me for now."

Martin walked through the house, checking that the sweet had gone from the broom cupboard. He looked for Rodrigo, who wasn't hard to find.

At the same time, Derek was trying to understand what was happening; he arranged to see Mrs Crier.

"You've got a nerve wanting to see me," she said to him when they met again in the waiting room on the way towards Fairy Land. "I told you never to make contact like this! Our deal does not give you the right to put me in this sort of danger. I wish we'd never met. I can't think why I came here in the first place."

"Calm down. We were meant to meet each other," said Derek. "I know what we agreed but my main duty is to protect the weak and vulnerable and that's what I am always going to do. These are not normal times and you have some information that will help me. What's going on in Louvain Terrace?"

"Look, this must never happen again. She is here, from Madrid, and nothing gets past her attention; she has spies everywhere. I've only come to tell you our agreement has ended and we can have no more contact." Mrs Crier was very nervous and agitated and kept looking around as if she was being watched.

Derek had little sympathy. "It wouldn't go well for you if it became known that during all these years you have been helping the Spiders because you wanted to become the number one Witch in London. I wonder what punishment potion you'd be given if I don't stay quiet about that?"

She said, "I don't know what I wanted. Power suddenly seemed important to me but I was never ambitious before. Listen, all I know is that Mrs Porter has gone and we Witches are being called down into the earth later this evening."

"Who is calling the meeting?" asked Derek.

"Lucy, of course. Lucy! She's here, in London, I told you," Mrs Crier was visibly shaking and clearly wanted to leave.

"I thought she'd come," said Derek. In fact, because the Supreme had appeared it wasn't really a surprise; all the Supers knew about Lucy. "I need to know what's going on in Louvain Terrace."

"All I can say is that Daisy is being targeted."

"What do you mean, targeted? How is that possible? There's a protective web all around the place and, thanks to Barry, especially around her."

"Too late. We're already inside that web."

"It's just not possible you can get near Daisy. There are Supers watching anything and everything near her. The security is too tight; Lucy couldn't get close enough to do any damage."

"Not Lucy, Mother. I've already said too much. I'm going," and that's just what she did, hurrying furtively away with a last remark. "We won't meet again; all my help is over. I have no ambition except survival."

"Mother?" repeated Derek to himself as he watched her leave, "Mother?" It made no sense.

Back in Louvain Terrace, Martin had found Rodrigo; he was, of course, with Daisy.

Martin waited. He needed Rodrigo alone but Daisy wouldn't put him down. Nor was that the only problem; Supers were everywhere and although Martin was known to them they didn't want him getting too close to Daisy. The instruction they had from Barry was that no one other than the family and Supers could be trusted.

After a couple of fruitless hours of watching and being watched, Martin went back to the kitchen to wait for Derek's return. He didn't have long to wait.

"Whatever the Witches are plotting, it's to do with that toy cat," he blurted out the instant Derek came through the curtain. "It's completely unnatural the way Daisy holds it all the time, and you don't know this but he gave me a sweet before and told me to lick it, but I didn't, I hid it and now it's gone. It must have contained some sort of spell but it doesn't yet seem to be causing any problems that I can see." This was all said at a breakneck pace; Martin couldn't wait to get it out.

Derek was of course a more advanced Spider than Martin and had been thinking about the information he'd heard from Mrs Crier. "You're right about a spell but my contact says it's to do with Mother. I haven't worked everything out completely, but perhaps the Witches are somehow using the toy cat to get at her, then somehow to Daisy and then to Barry; that could be what's really going on. I remember that episode in the warehouse where Daisy was used as bait; the Witches always like to confuse us as to their real intentions."

"It can't involve Mother," said Martin breathing deeply and

calming down a fraction, "she would never, ever hurt or threaten a single hair on Daisy's head, nor on anyone's head come to that. You must have this wrong. Maybe that contact you went to see has misled you as part of their real plan."

"Hmmm, maybe so," mused Derek thoughtfully; it was a point. "I suppose that's possible."

He looked hard at Martin, "You do realise, of course, that in the ultimate, we may need to sacrifice Daisy to the Witches. Our responsibility must be to save and protect Barry because he can do the greater good. He would never agree so we must, all of us, be prepared if it comes to it, to kidnap Barry as best we all can, get him away to a place of safety and leave his people-family to sort themselves out. Who knows, perhaps we'd be able to come back later and help them?"

Martin stared hard at Derek. The reality of the situation was becoming very frightening.

Derek took a deep breath, "In the meantime there's a meeting I have to attend."

It was many long years since Derek had been underground in the Great Hall and it hadn't been a very enjoyable experience. He never thought he'd be back there again and certainly didn't want to be. The clammy, dry cold was intense, and the whole place had a sort of evil smell that was very hard to explain when it didn't exist anywhere else. This was the Witches' Chamber in London, a deep chasm where they could meet, or bring the children whose minds they had captured before sending them to Geneva.

Lucy was floating in the air and underneath her were 200 or

so London-based Witches. Over to one side, at a lower respectful height, someone else was hovering. Lucy pointed at her.

"This is Mary," she said. "She is my tried and trusted second in command; you may also have heard of her. She controls South America for me and I've called her to London because the situation we face is so important. She's going to say a few words."

With that Lucy floated down and Mary floated up to take the controlling height.

"Listen, Witches," Mary began, "we are facing our biggest challenge. I can confirm to you all that the Supreme Spider is in London and all the Supers are also either here or on their way. The Supreme is living with a family in Louvain Terrace; some of you know his name already, Barry. Spiders have waited for him over many generations. He is receiving Revelations by the day and has taken the step of stopping any of them being released, so our reference books are not being updated. We cannot react to The Chronicles when we don't know what they say and so this is a serious disadvantage."

She paused for breath and continued, "For a while we have thought Barry was the Supreme. You will all have heard the Magic Song and it takes a very important Spider to write something like that. So we have been making plans to deal with him. Mrs Porter was a fool. She could not see past her own pitiful ambition. The plan she put in place to eliminate Barry, and take over from Lucy, was so basic and unimaginative that I actually found it hard to believe. However, we now control her spell and put it to some use, so moves are under way within Louvain Terrace to turn things to our advantage. The Spiders have thought their protective web would keep us out but we are already inside."

Lucy and Mary switched heights again as the Witches cheered. Lucy looked down at them and said, "We know everything in this world and you should remember that nothing happens, beyond the actions of a very few Spiders, unless we wish it. Yet there is someone here who, for some time, has forgotten what it means to be a Witch. I have allowed her to remain with us in case I might find further opportunities to turn her weakness to our advantage by planting more false hopes or information in her mind, but those times are now past."

She floated down and gave Mrs Crier a punishment potion and, as with Mrs Pugh and Mrs Porter, she never features again. As he looked on, Derek felt no sympathy for her. You see how the pursuit of self-interest will always prove to be an undoing; loyalty is the greatest of qualities.

"Now, the rest of you stay ready because the great battle is ahead. The Spiders will prepare but as things stand they cannot defeat us," and with that Mary and Lucy drifted away to make plans of their own.

In Louvain Terrace, Mother's hand was tingling more than ever; she shook it vigorously but it made no difference.

"What are you doing that for?" said Father looking curiously at her.

"Oh, I don't know, anyway I wanted to talk to you about Daisy. I was thinking, perhaps we should send her to that finishing school the nice lady told us about."

"What?" Father thought he must be hearing things. "You can't be serious. We talked about this and decided it was a complete non-starter. We can't send Daisy away with people we know nothing about."

"Yes, I know we discussed it earlier, but the lady explained all the benefits and I'm worried that we're just being selfish by saying Daisy can't better herself. If you had heard about the opportunities then I really think you'd see things differently. We both only want the best for our daughter and I can't believe you would deny her the chance of a lifetime. Something like this will never be on offer again because the school is looking out right now for certain children of Daisy's age."

Mother was starting to be sure this would be for the best. People can fool themselves into believing what they want, or are told, to believe.

Father could see that this was a serious matter. He thought for a moment.

"If you really think it's a good idea then perhaps you should invite her back for me to meet. We could include Daisy too and see what she thinks," he said reluctantly, "but I must say I'll take some convincing."

The Spiders had been listening and when Derek returned from the underground meeting of the Witches, Martin explained how Daisy could be sent into the care of Lucy.

Derek didn't seem as surprised or concerned as Martin had expected; in fact he seemed very calm about it and was more inclined to concentrate on the conversations he had heard underground. Spiders, and most people, like to think that they personally have the important grasp of what should be done and what is important.

"I knew from the last time I went to the Great Hall using some, what shall I say, powers I could borrow from another world, that I could stay unseen by Witches. I never realised I'd need them again. I'd forgotten how cold it is down there. Lucy is definitely in London with her helper, Mary. They have got rid of Mrs Crier, Mrs Pugh and Mrs Porter, who had spun a spell against us. They got some use out of it though, and they are definitely already inside our protective web."

Derek continued, "That's the important thing, they have penetrated our external shield and are inside the web."

He looked at Martin's face and realised he should also say something about the possibility of Daisy leaving.

"Don't worry, I'm sure we'll be able to stop that school stuff happening when Barry gets back. Anyway, Mother and Father would never actually agree to send Daisy away."

However, in advance of Lucy's visit, Mother had already mentioned the school idea to Daisy and it was certainly clear she wanted to go, as long as Rodrigo went with her.

In their underground chamber Lucy and Mary were reviewing progress.

"It's all going nicely to plan," said Mary. "Those stupid Spiders Barry left behind to look after things will now concentrate on stopping us getting at Daisy but they're too late, thanks to your touching spells. They will never see our true intention by looking elsewhere. Only Barry can cause us a problem but he already has other things on his mind and his difficulties are set to increase."

Lucy said, "I hope Derek reports our meeting accurately; he didn't seem at all concerned about poor Mrs Crier. He thinks I cannot smell him when he is near and imagines I don't know his location when he tries to hide. He talks to the Fairies but doesn't understand he's really talking with me. He is a fool who didn't know Mrs Crier was completely in my power."

Then she frowned, "However, none of that is important when compared to The Chronicles. I know Barry is receiving many Revelations and none are being released. It's completely out of order. How can we adjust when we don't know what new teaching has been understood? All I've been able to do is place a confusion spell in the minds of the Spiders but I cannot be sure if it will work because Barry has so many powers. We must get our reactions to the Revelations."

Little did Lucy know that the confusion spell could be working better than she thought. Derek and Martin were nowhere near understanding all that was happening and there was now no agreed plan of defence around Louvain Terrace. They had been relying on a protective web that was already breached.

In the hidden wood near Derek's house, Barry could not fathom his way through the references to Fairy Land. He knew he needed to mix existing paragraphs with the new Revelations, but so far he'd had no success.

He still suspected it all rested on the Unnumbered.

13.

Lucy Calls Again

Barry stared at the three Unnumbered. One of them was longer than the others.

"It is foolish to question what has been provided and so it must be explained why the same tree presents itself differently when approached from a different direction. The importance of this understanding would be that it requires no understanding because every traveller carries their own experience and destiny; it cannot be transferred. This is not to say why each tree must change when approached but rather that all trees are always changing, even when unnoticed. It should be added that those more advanced on a journey will look at less of the tree but see it more clearly."

Barry thought about it, then he thought about it some more, remembering one of the early solutions he needed to find from a time far less complicated. There were moments when he felt the meaning contained within the words was becoming clear and with just a few more little bits of clarity it might all make sense, but then a murky fog appeared. When would understanding ever require no understanding?

At the same time, Mother was looking at the card Lucy had left behind; it was unlike any other because it carried an attraction spell and so could not be ignored. It also helped plant ideas into the minds of all those to whom it was given and had told Mother she should see Lucy again.

Lucy had explained that it wasn't a calling card at all but an answering card and so, until the family were clients of the school, it would not provide the usual contact details. Rather, when Mother wanted to speak with Lucy it would simply show how to do it at that particular time. Lucy was currently in London so the card only showed a local telephone number; Mother called it.

"Lovely to hear from you, Mrs Davies. How can I help?"

Lucy was being as nice as pie.

"Oh hello, Lucy. Well, my husband and I were talking and we thought that perhaps it would be a good idea to learn a little bit more about the possibilities of sending Daisy to your school. We are not committing yet mind, we've got more questions, but at least if you did come round it would give my husband a chance to meet you."

"Of course, how very sensible." Lucy had noticed the word "yet," and how Mother mentioned her husband twice in a couple of sentences. If she'd actually wanted to take Daisy away to Geneva then clearly Father would also need to agree. However, it didn't really matter; it was enough if she could fool Barry into thinking it did. That would make him vulnerable and help Lucy get the reactions she desperately needed to update the *Witches Reference Books.*

She also couldn't help but like the idea that the Spiders' protective web was in place to keep her out but she had made it useless by causing Mother to ask her in. The web had no power to block Mother's wishes.

Lucy told Mary about her invitation back to Louvain Terrace.

"That's all very well, I suppose, but what's the purpose of going there?" asked Mary.

"You'll see," said Lucy with a thin smile. There were spells Mary didn't know.

Many Spider eyes were looking at Lucy as she rang the bell, shook hands with Mother and Father and was invited inside. The Supers were not at all happy that their biggest enemy could walk so openly through the protective web into the very home they were guarding. They would have been even more unhappy if they had known that the touching spell had **just** been triggered; the sweet had prepared the opportunity and now Lucy had taken it.

In the kitchen Martin said, "It's outrageous. How on earth could Lucy be in the next room? I'm only glad Barry isn't here to see it."

"I'd like to say it's not important, but I think there's more going on here than the obvious. Why is she here? Let me go over every detail of the past 24 hours and see if I can spot something. Lucy is their equivalent to Barry so she is not to be underestimated," said

Derek. His senses were telling him that Martin might have been right to highlight Rodrigo as a key factor in the Witches' plan.

It was clear to Lucy as she sat down in the living room with Father and Mother that Spider eyes and ears were all around her. Every word said would be noted and analysed so care was needed, but she was the first Witch ever to enter 14 Louvain Terrace and it was something she could use to her advantage.

"We thought we'd start without Daisy," said Father trying to take charge. "She can join us later, if it seems worthwhile." He tried to emphasise the "if."

"Would you like a cup of tea, Lucy?" asked Mother, much more aware of hospitality.

Father answered, "I wouldn't mind," seemingly totally unaware that the question was directed elsewhere.

Lucy smiled. "No thank you, Mrs Davies. I find it disagrees with me; nothing at all, thank you."

Mother sat down next to Father.

"So," grimaced Father after realising that no tea was coming his way, "I appreciate you've spoken to my wife about this before, but just for my benefit, would you mind going over it again?"

"Not at all," said Lucy and she told her tale.

The parents called Daisy, who came downstairs clutching Rodrigo. She didn't seem to be listening to anything being said, yet when Father stopped talking for a moment after explaining matters as he saw them, she said, "We want to go, don't we?" and she gazed at the cuddly toy looking back at her as if he would answer.

"Can I go back upstairs now, please?" she asked.

Mother and Father looked at each other; their daughter seemed very keen on the idea.

It was time for Lucy to say a few words.

"Before you go, Daisy, there is one thing that I have to tell your parents. You see, before we take any young boy or girl onto this…" and she paused, "…very, very special life-changing course we have to know that the child is right for us. In the same way, you have to be sure the course is right for your child. It means that we must firstly have Daisy with us for a weekend at our preparatory school in Hampshire. I hope it won't be a problem but it's a matter of our Foundation rules; I'm sure you understand," and she looked inquiringly at them both.

"What do you think, Daisy?" asked Mother.

"I've said to you before," she repeated, "we want to go," and Daisy went back upstairs leaving the three of them to talk.

"I don't suppose a weekend would do any harm, just to see. If Daisy isn't suitable or if she doesn't like it then we don't have to go ahead," said Mother to Father.

"But we don't know anything about these people, or this school; no disrespect intended," Father replied, glancing at Lucy. He felt determined to make the point.

Lucy simply gestured as if it was the wisest thing ever said; however, the sign said the matter was non-negotiable.

"Yes, but you have met this lovely lady now and you can see it's all respectable," said Mother, squeezing Father's hand.

"Oh well, I suppose it might be for the best," he suddenly heard himself say.

Lucy gave her brightest smile. "Good, I have an idea. Today

is Friday and I'm driving down to the school straight after this meeting. If it's convenient, you could quickly pack a bag for Daisy and she can come with me. I'll bring her back on Sunday and we can talk again then."

You will appreciate that in normal circumstances Daisy would be going nowhere. However, there was nothing normal about the current events in Louvain Terrace. Mother, and now Father, had been affected by the touching spell and Daisy was under the control of Rodrigo. Super Spiders were everywhere but nonetheless, the upshot was that when Lucy left the house, Daisy and Rodrigo went with her.

The Supers were frustrated and helpless because the touching spell stopped them planting better, wiser thoughts about the school in the minds of Mother and Father. Also the idea was such a surprise development they were taken somewhat off guard, but the absolute truth of the matter was that they were less concerned with what might happen to Daisy. Derek had made clear that Barry was their top priority, so they watched as the black car, with a number plate GCHQ 1 visible only to Supers and Witches, disappeared down the road.

"Barry will just have to understand we are concerned with the greater good," said Derek. "This goes beyond Daisy."

Martin wasn't so sure. "He won't see it like that. We may be acting with the finest of intentions but Daisy is in his people-family and he will go absolutely mental to learn that we've allowed Lucy to take her away."

Martin was right. Barry had sought a quiet remote place in the hidden forest to make sense of the Fairies, the new Revelations, cross-referencing and the Unnumbered but he suddenly now had an overwhelming sense that all was not well in Louvain Terrace and Daisy was involved.

He immediately came home by web-thread and, on finding out what had happened, was as angry as a Supreme is allowed to be.

Speaking very quietly and calmly he said, "You mean to tell me that Lucy was allowed into my family home, to speak with Mother and Father and then leave, taking Daisy with her? Is that what you're telling me?"

"That's about it," said Derek reluctantly, "but you must appreciate, although our protective web was in place, it couldn't work because Mother invited Lucy inside. Then, for a reason we don't yet know about, Daisy wanted to leave. Although we're pretty sure that was something to do with the toy cat; and for another different reason we know nothing about, Mother and Father also seemed happy and even excited that Daisy should go. All the Supers were ready to intervene if we'd understood what was happening but we didn't and the truth is, and I'm sorry to say this, one child is not important when compared with your safety – you are the Supreme Spider."

"If I were like the GCHQ, I'd be giving you a punishment potion you'd never forget for allowing Daisy to be taken away. Lately, I have been learning some valuable lessons that I realise were needed before understanding The Chronicles. However, make no mistake, it is not acceptable to me that you put any of my people-family at risk. I'm not concerned about the greater good when I think of Daisy, so perhaps that's something else The Chronicles will need to be making clear in my education. Now leave me alone. I must think about what to do next."

Barry snuggled down into his little bed in the kitchen. When he was younger it had been the place he was most content. He was still angry and concerned but had to consider things calmly, even though he felt under extreme pressure because he couldn't let anything happen to Daisy. Yet within a minute he saw shapes of Lucy, Daisy and Rodrigo floating as if in Fairy Land.

Lucy had realised that their lack of reactions was in fact absolutely critical; the situation simply had to be corrected. The Witches needed to know how to respond to Revelations. Knowledge provides the most power, don't forget, so a change in her plans became necessary.

She had originally thought that taking Daisy prisoner would cause the Spiders total confusion. In those circumstances she could at least have some degree of control over Barry. However she realised that wouldn't be as important as receiving new information into the *Witches Reference Books.*

In any event, some time ago she had prepared an alternative future plan, so it wasn't very difficult to decide what needed to be done next. She could dispense totally with all the spells currently active on Mother and Father. They were no longer needed; Lucy thought another better ending was available.

She made Barry an offer.

He heard her voice as if she was speaking through a cloud. "So you are the Supreme. Well, I have no need of conversation but listen carefully to every word I say. The Revelations must all immediately be released. I know you have received them. If they are, Daisy will be safely returned overnight to your family, completely unharmed, and the spells currently active in and around Louvain Terrace will be removed. Should you not agree, then Daisy will be lost forever. If she returns she will not remember anything of her time with me. You know I can be trusted on this," and the shapes faded away.

Barry immediately called Derek and Martin back into the kitchen. He explained what had happened; they were both in no doubt about what must be done.

Derek said, "Of course you are the Supreme and so we cannot do more than give you our best advice, but there was a reason you stopped the release of the Revelations and it must still apply. This cannot be just about Daisy. It's natural you feel upset because she belonged to your people-family but you must consider the greater good. Since time began we have lived by and through The Chronicles and believed in their teachings. This includes the ongoing Missing guidance we get from The Revelations to complete gaps and explain developments, and there are certainly more things to be understood. Only you will be shown these; that cannot be put at risk."

He paused. "Daisy is, and I'm sorry to say it again, unimportant. The Witches have been our mortal enemies throughout the years, but we have all been waiting for this moment when you and the GCHQ both walk the earth. Now we will see battle joined and good triumph over evil. The stakes are much higher than any single child."

Martin agreed. "I'm not even a Super but I can see Derek's right. You may think we made mistakes in letting Lucy anywhere near Louvain Terrace, but the address and occupants are only important to you because of a time now past. You must move on and accept the new place and role you occupy, plus the responsibilities that come with it."

Barry wasn't happy.

"Firstly, never again say to me Daisy 'belonged' to my people-family, she 'belongs' in it and always will. You both tell me nothing new or say anything other than the expected. It is honest advice but unwelcome and useless; there are times when these go together."

Barry walked a little way up and down before continuing, "I fully recognise my responsibility as the Supreme Spider. It means you cannot be my friends, they can be chosen, but my family is forever and that fact is unchanging, at least to me."

Later in the evening Barry released the Revelations and so all over the world The Chronicles updated. At the end of each chapter, except the last, a Draw line appeared. The Witches immediately received every reaction bar one.

You see, there was a consequence Lucy had set in motion, and it was very important. For the first time the Witches were given recommendations to some Revelations the Spiders had not yet understood; many of the most important were still underlined. It meant that potentially Witches could at last move ahead in their battle for supremacy over the hearts and minds of young children.

However, Lucy soon encountered similar difficulties to those Barry had faced; some of the reactions were not only complex but also relied on a degree of cross-referencing for best effect. It would take time for her as the GCHQ to think things through.

She was also unaware of the three Unnumbered paragraphs. They were of a different nature because they were unreferenced and could not therefore update corresponding paragraphs in the *Witches Reference Books*. Barry felt no need to mention them. He had done everything asked of him by releasing all the Revelations.

Daisy came home early the next morning. The doorbell rang and she was there alone: safe, sound and carrying Rodrigo. Mother's hand no longer tingled because she and Father had been released from both the touching spell and the answering card spell.

Mother hugged Daisy very tightly. "I've absolutely no idea what I was thinking about. How on earth could I possibly have done something so stupid? I'll never forgive myself for sending you away with that woman. I must have been temporarily insane but today I feel my usual self again. Can you ever forgive me?" she asked.

"I didn't mind," Daisy said, holding Rodrigo closely.

Father interrupted, "It was me, too. I didn't intend agreeing with any of it. I was just humouring you both really up to then, but Daisy you were happy to go and Mother, you seemed so certain. I still wasn't going to support the idea but suddenly I could hear my voice making sounds of approval. I couldn't stop; it was so weird. It just came across as the right thing to say at the time. Words are such funny things."

Barry was being extremely watchful of everything connected with the family and, although Lucy completely kept her promise, he noted she had added something by returning Rodrigo.

So after Daisy's safe arrival home, Barry firstly adjusted the protective web around Louvain Terrace, ensuring that no new spells whatsoever could be brought into the house; but having Rodrigo already inside wouldn't do at all. However, because Barry was by now in full control of his powers it was a problem he could soon fix.

In fact, Barry felt that Lucy was somewhat challenging him by sending Rodrigo back to Louvain Terrace because she must have known it would be unacceptable. Anyway, as the cat's eyes turned from blue to black and slowly closed, Daisy lost all interest in cuddly toys. That evening she put Rodrigo in the broom cupboard and never touched him again.

Now that his people-family were all safe, Barry could look to the future. He called a council of war with all his senior commanders and made a short speech.

"Now it begins. Many lives have been spent preparing for this moment: you, me and every Spider that has come before and watches us now. It is our greatest test but we have good on our side. Outside of Spider Land the world turns unaware but it is a different place. Bad things happen all the time and even as we speak, in another part of London a great and bold enemy is preparing to do harm, and it is we Spiders they must overcome if their aims are to be achieved. The Chronicles will always give us an advantage but they cannot be used before they are understood. I have already learned in my short time as the Supreme that I have not been ready or able to lead us into the fight. The deficit must be remedied and very soon it will be."

14.

Barry Makes a Decision

The second Unnumbered passage stared back at Barry in the same unyielding way as the others.

"There is no before nor after but only the now when you are able to be. Your actions become part of the whole so they are not everything, there is always more. To reach the intended you must therefore go outside all that is shown and heard, using trust in what will be found."

Not far away Lucy was studying the reactions. They were, of course, directed towards the success of evil over good, and traditionally provided the means for the Witches to survive and prosper in balance to The Chronicles. Lucy had correctly understood that they were always of paramount importance, and now the Witches were in possession of recommended reactions before the Spiders had understood, and could therefore properly use the original teachings. If such knowledge was marshalled quickly it marked a significant reversal in the balance of power.

Every few hours the Spider high command was getting together to consider the latest information being gathered; it was the time to do so. It was why the Supers were in London, to be there as and when they were needed by the Supreme.

"I still haven't understood all the meanings I have been shown." Barry was somewhat ashamed to admit it; he knew the expectation of everyone. The Revelations had been released but many remained underlined and were confusing, so the Spiders waited for his interpretation. Only he knew about, and had access to, the Unnumbered.

"I will understand them though," he added, sounding much more confident than he felt. "Anyway, apart from finally mastering The Chronicles, or not, where are we?"

The question was asked because the battle soon to be joined would affect all creatures. Traditionally, as you have heard before, Spiders have good allies and friends in the ants whereas Witches get along better with cats and most things that fly. Yet this would be war conducted on a much bigger scale; none could stand aside.

Derek reported back, "As expected the alliances are splitting about 50/50. We are doing well in the cities but the countryside and jungles are mostly with the Witches. Don't worry, it's always been like that; when it comes to the crunch some creatures are usually against us, but there are others we can count on."

"If I could only get things right then a giant head-to-head battle can be avoided because I know The Chronicles provide answers to mean there is nothing to fight over. Look, you keep making plans, but my plan is that there is no need for a plan because there will be no need for a fight."

Barry was sure he would be given a different and better way to defeat the Witches.

In the meanwhile there was something wrong, and Barry knew what it was.

He had let his family down and needed to put things right. So that night when Mother was sleeping he planted a very special dream in her head.

He had thought a lot about what to say. Eventually it seemed to him that the best thing would be to tell her mostly everything, just as it had happened. So she was told about Spiders, Secret Spiders, Super Secrets and the Supreme Secret followed by the eternal battle they were waging with Witches, then the incredible news that here in Louvain Terrace was the Supreme Secret Spider, Barry. The very same little Spider who wrote the Magic Song for the family to understand there was no need to be afraid of them.

Yet that song had brought dangers to the house because it revealed who he was and the Witches couldn't then allow Barry to grow and become more powerful through Revelations. The immediate danger had manifested itself in Daisy. It was Barry's fault she had been taken away by Lucy and although he had ensured a safe and speedy return, unharmed in any way, he felt very guilty that it had happened in the first place. He wanted to say he was extremely sorry and it would never happen again; from now on they would all be kept secure.

When Mother woke up she felt full of warmth and sympathy for Spiders in general and Barry in particular, even if, as with all dreams, not everything could be recalled. She went straight to the kitchen where Barry was talking to Derek and Martin and pulled back the curtain to where he was speaking. She wasn't afraid and spoke directly to him.

"You are one of our family now, little Spider, and on behalf of us all I want to say that it is we who should be sorry for treating you so badly. We cannot know what you know or what you can be, but I will at least try harder not to hurt or frighten any of you ever again."

I should underline at this point how difficult it is for Spiders to understand the feelings other creatures have, especially humans. The bond that can exist between friends, and especially within families, simply doesn't happen in Spider Land; they have a different approach. Spiders knew of some really powerful external force, often very clearly evident, but it was just regarded as a mystery applicable elsewhere and played no part, and could play no part, in their daily lives.

However, the night before had been the first time a dream of this nature, explaining all that needed to be explained, had been planted by The Supreme. In consequence it was as powerful as the Magic Song because it also worked in reverse to mean that, through her response and what he could feel in her mind, Barry could understand something of what a family can be. He and Mother had communicated in a very deep sense and he felt a new dimension to an ordinary concept of life. There is much more in the world than can be imagined.

"What on earth was that all about?" said Derek after Mother had left. "It really seemed like you were one of the people-family."

"It was unbelievable," said Martin also looking at Barry in wonder. "These are strange times to be sure. You are certainly the Supreme Spider."

Barry said, "I'm at last beginning to understand what it really means," and refused the chance to be more specific.

"So anyway, let's get back to the urgent business before us," said Derek impatiently. "We have been studying the Revelations you released, but coming to different conclusions as to their meanings. It's fairly useless information to us when they are still underlined, like mine is I might add. We need your guidance to understand everything, but at least I can see that I was never going to travel beyond the waiting room to Fairy Land. It wasn't a waiting room for me at all actually, more as far as I was going to get."

Barry gave a little laugh. "My guidance? Well, I hope you're not holding your breath. With regard to your Revelation, I said before that it was complex; I still haven't quite got it myself. When something like that hasn't arrived, it's because of travelling too slowly. You tried understanding something you were not to know at that time. The Chronicles don't say we can enter any of the other worlds, even if we are told they exist. Fairies must live in their own allotted place watching us, and maybe sometimes we can watch them, but we can never live where we are not meant to be, and nor can they. This world is our home."

Barry wondered what the Fairies would be thinking right now.

They might want to help; after all, they'd have no love of Witches, but what could they do? He realised the idea that Fairies would provide answers was false. Derek had not understood the Revelation he was given because he wanted to read into it much more than it conveyed. His commitment and enthusiasm had even influenced Barry into looking for answers outside The Chronicles. That error was why the Underlining had not disappeared for Derek, who was given all he needed at a certain point but wanted more. In contrast Barry was slowly beginning to see and accept that the answers he was seeking as the Supreme would only be presented when he showed he was ready to receive them.

Derek was visibly disappointed to learn that on this point he had not proceeded wisely.

Barry was sympathetic and said, "Look Derek, even though you are one of our highest-rated Supers, it's pointless for you or anyone else to study and try to interpret all that is revealed when it is incomplete. I am here at this time because this is my time, not yours or that of anybody else and I think I am approaching the moment when I alone will be given the key to unlock the great secret within The Chronicles. We must all accept that the future's ahead and it's not coming too soon."

Barry asked them to leave; he wanted to consider what he should do next.

"How about the protective web?" said Martin as he was going. "Shall we keep it in place?"

"No, there's no point. It wasn't any help in dealing with the GCHQ. I may have underestimated Lucy but at least I'm sure the Witches cannot win, even if I'm still completely unsure how they're going to lose. Keep all the Supers here though. The Chronicles called them to me so they may still be needed for some purpose. I just don't know what it is yet."

Barry was left alone with his thoughts.

Underground, Lucy and Mary were studying their *Witches Reference Books.*

"You're not making sense," said Mary. "The Chronicles update and we then receive guidance telling us how best to respond. It's always been that way, action followed by reaction. So what do you mean by saying the order has been reversed? It's impossible."

Lucy looked worried, a weight was on her mind.

"Yes, and I made that happen," she said. "More to the point, we have gained a significant potential advantage. Don't you see? The Chronicles are reaching a point of completion where their greatest truth will be available. We will then become powerless and that moment is close. More Revelations have been sent in the past few days than in the previous centuries, but for a while we have answers to teachings the Spiders have not yet understood. That must be a powerful weapon if we can use it quickly."

"Why quickly?" asked Mary.

"Think about it. As you say, the Chronicles yield a Revelation and when it's understood and in use by the Spiders we get the reaction telling us what to do in return. That has been how the world keeps in balance; everyone knows what's happening. Then the Supreme arrived, here in London. I left Madrid and made him release all the Revelations he'd been given, whether understood or not. So now at this moment, and because of that, we could have more knowledge than the Spiders."

"So what?" said Mary. "You're saying it's only a potential."

Lucy was pacing around. She ignored that comment and was thinking hard as she spoke. "The Chronicles are evolving to reach completion but I sense that will require new information, not Revelations. Barry is being given those extra teachings and we can have no knowledge of them. We would be told nothing in order to react to what? I could think about it for years and be no wiser. Yet it means The Chronicles are assuming I will now wait and see what Barry does next," and she paused meaningfully, "but what if they're wrong? Our response at that time would be the final act between us; one step behind the Spiders and again at a disadvantage. However, suppose we can use information gained from the reactions already in our reference books? What if I can understand what they say before Barry understands what The Chronicles are telling him. It might be our only opportunity to change the future to our advantage."

Mary looked confused. It was a lot of information to absorb but she did at least realise that the Witches must wait.

Lucy, however was studying hard, seeking important meanings in the time when reaction remained ahead of action. In the kitchen Barry stared at the third and final Unnumbered. A wild thought entered his head and it wouldn't go away, just like the music of the Magic Song.

"What?" asked Derek looking at him.

"I'm not sure; I shall have to think some more," answered Barry.

"OK, but what is it?" said Derek, as nosey as ever.

"It's not for you," and Barry left the kitchen.

"What's all that about?" Martin said to Derek.

"I don't know, but we have to trust Barry to get to the bottom of The Chronicles. We should concentrate on how we can help, and that's by waiting here for him to get back." Thus the Witches were waiting and the Spiders waited.

In the living room Father and Mother were discussing her dream. "It certainly sounds strange," Father said. "I don't seem able to remember any of mine but that one has stuck with you, hasn't it?"

Mother reflected, "It wasn't a normal dream. It came to me in that way but it was actually more of a message and it came from a Spider. I know it sounds absolutely mad but I think it was from the one who taught us the song about their legs. We talked together and he was helping me understand why we agreed to send Daisy away with that woman – if that's what I should call her. I've been so unhappy about what we did and needed to make some better sense of it."

"I've been unhappy about that too, you know," said Father. "I was going to say Daisy's going nowhere and then, in the blink of an eye, I was packing her overnight bag. Why hasn't the Spider come and explained it to me?"

Poor Father, he had no idea that he had been helpless to

resist the idea of Daisy leaving because of the influence exercised through the touching spell, passed on to him by Mother when they were together with Lucy.

Mother then heard herself say something she didn't understand, "Dreams are watertight when they stay the night; as you rise, it's a compromise." She wondered where those words had come from, and continued with a puzzled expression on her brow, "I don't know. I was the one he sang to so maybe he's more comfortable with women?" She smiled at Father. "Anyway, it doesn't matter; he has told me what has been happening and I have told you, but it's not over yet." She lowered her voice to a whisper. "Those poor small Spiders are trying to save us from those wicked things. I do worry for them and it's our Spider who is at the forefront of it all. "

"There are people out there who would think you've gone totally and completely out of your mind. Fancy going to speak with a Spider when you wake up? It does sound crazy." Father still found it all a mystery.

"I don't care. I know when I have to say something. It seemed very important at the time and not only that, it was absolutely necessary. I just know it," Mother looked somewhat sheepish and added, "although I don't understand why."

Daisy came into the lounge with her big sister Jessica. She was back to her normal happy self and Mother and Father had made the decision not to mention any of this to her. Childhood is above all an opportunity to be children. Even at 15, although Jessica felt she was grown up, such things don't happen by that age; it takes time for the right wiring to connect in the brain.

That day the family had a lovely time, playing games together, talking and watching television. When Mother went to bed she would dream again of friendly, happy, useful little Spiders.

Both Lucy and Barry had been preparing for what lay ahead. Nothing had been resolved with regard to either The Chronicles or the Unnumbered, yet in the morning Barry was certain about what he must do.

"I still haven't made every connection," he told Martin before Derek arrived, "but I have made a decision after finally realising that nothing can exist out of turn. Things happen when it is their time to happen. The Revelations from within The Missing come when they're necessary but then it's up to us to understand them. Why should it be different with the Unnumbered? In other words, I'm wasting my time trying to figure out any endings, because they won't appear until they are due to appear; that's what The Chronicles teach in 14/14. What I must do is trust in the circumstances when they will be shown."

Martin looked completely puzzled.

"The Unnumbered? I'm really worried Barry. Are things meant to be as complicated as this? What if you've got it all wrong, and you're just simply throwing away the hopes and dreams of every Spider by some misguided thinking. I certainly don't read 14/14 as offering a great clue about some essential message hidden within The Chronicles and scheduled to pop up one day," he said.

However Barry was now certain.

"This is bigger than Spiders. If I'm right I must go alone to the underground Witches' hall. I know it puts me in great danger but there the final truth will be shown."

He continued, "Listen Martin, it never seems to have been noticed but there is a word mentioned only once in The Chronicles and the Unnumbered. I thought in my vanity that, "for amongst many there is one alone to guide the way," was referring to me, but it wasn't. It's just a single word to find but words have hidden meanings. Sometimes they deceive you so the meanings are to be found if understanding is to follow. The number of words used determines what can be explained."

Barry looked thoughtful. It was obvious he had something very important to say on this point.

Martin waited patiently until Barry spoke again. "You must remember The Chronicles have been written specifically with Witches in mind. Apart from teachings about day-to-day living they contain the reason confirming absolutely why good must, and will, overcome evil. I need to look beyond what I see and hear to find the key unlocking the knowledge that is required. When that proof is revealed then faith becomes understanding and the Witches can have no further involvement in this world."

Martin wasn't impressed. "Was that it? Well, I still have no idea what you're talking about. One single word tells you so much? Seems strange to me, and what on earth are the Unnumbered? As far as all these interpretations are concerned then I'll leave that to you as the Supreme to work out but I can see your plan is too dangerous. What if

The Chronicles already provide you with everything necessary to find the answers we seek? This connection stuff and the numbers game could perhaps be rubbish. If all the Supers were with you underground then maybe you'd be safe, but by yourself you'll be frozen and perish."

Barry answered, "No, you must remember it can only be me; no other Spiders. Don't forget what I said about timing and what must be done. In the past the Witches have never understood anything before us. They get reactions, updates, responses, call them whatever you like, to the teachings of The Chronicles but not to the Unnumbered. They are the key to unlocking the greatest truth, and only I see them. It means the understanding we seek will be revealed to me but cannot be explained," and Barry paused for a moment.

"I am the means to give the Witches a reaction that does not begin with a Revelation. I haven't understood everything yet because it's not been my time to do so but at least I think I now see when that time will arrive. It has been travelling slowly but that's because of needing to wait until a search becomes the answer. Anyway the long and the short of it all is that the Witches are waiting to see what can be learnt from the teachings I am being shown outside of The Chronicles."

"Well, I don't understand what's happening and that's for sure, but I really do wish you'd stop saying 'the Unnumbered' because it means nothing to me and frankly sounds ridiculous. I do know Derek will not let you go underground by yourself."

Barry replied, "Ha, sorry. Don't worry about the Unnumbered because they are something you never have to be concerned with. As regards to Derek, he won't worry either because I won't tell him. Only I can reach outside all that has been shown or heard to know the intended."

"I've absolutely no idea what you're talking about!" said Martin.

This is perhaps a good time to confirm that the word mentioned once in The Spider Chronicles and the Unnumbered is also used only once throughout this telling of Barry and his adventures. There are clues as to what it might be but, should your curiosity be aroused, it must of course be sought not gifted.

In your quest, remember that a word or phrase may seem strange, out of place and perhaps irrelevant, but every word sends a message to somebody; as can those omitted. Most of the words you are reading have been used in other places; it is purely their order and context that gives rise to the particular meanings, images, questions and thoughts now placed before you. It proves that connections are all important because alongside one there is another; combined they have the ability to change everything.

Underground, Lucy suddenly smiled to herself.

"He's coming here," she told Mary.

"What?" said Mary.

"Barry, he's coming here, all alone. I don't know what he's thinking, but I will say that he's a very brave little Spider."

15.

The End Is Where It Appears

Barry had never been underground before so it was one thing deciding to go to the Witches' hall but quite another to do it. Neither did he want to involve Derek in the journey, but Barry knew how to get there, he'd ask the ants; when they were on a march they got everywhere.

"I wouldn't go," said a local commander in the garden. "There's all sorts of funny happenings when you get as deeply down into the earth as that; it's a different place altogether. The ants who live there are a strange bunch, always mumbling to themselves. I've been below on a patrol or two and I can't make out what they're saying. It probably comes from listening to the Spellbound; that's what we call them anyway. People who spend their time dancing around and chanting for hours on end, working themselves up into a frenzy. It's not natural, and they sometimes keep children up with them half the night – not that they know it's night-time of course. Black as anything down there except for some torches. No, if I were you I'd stay well clear."

"Thanks for all the advice but I have to go, so just tell me how to best get down there, please," and because it was Barry and the next stage was under way then, that's just what the ants did; like Spanner had said, they were ready.

The tunnels they needed to travel weren't made for Spiders but with the garden ants showing the way, Barry reached the underground hall, the biggest chamber he'd ever seen. A large table was in the middle; chairs were around it with dark passages leading to who knows where. The lighting was supplied by torches burning on the walls, although in the middle a few candles also pierced the gloom. Barry could barely make out the shapes shuffling about.

"This is as far as we go," said the commander, and the ants reversed their steps back up into the cool, clear, fresh air.

Barry was left alone in the semi-black and clammy cold. The dream he had once planted in Jessica's mind about being prepared and grasping opportunities suddenly came into his head. That had been what now seemed like a very long time ago and certainly well before he recognised himself as the Supreme Secret, but for some reason he started thinking about the messages contained in that dream. Barry always wanted to help others, but now the teacher needed to understand the teachings.

He felt very calm and somehow in control of the situation, even though he was just one small Spider in the midst of many Witches intent on doing him harm. The unexpected was now expected. Barry felt sure the Unnumbered would be explained, with all the cross-references associated together for a full meaning of the greatest truth.

The Chronicles completed and evil defeated! It was such an exciting prospect.

Yet, as Barry awaited developments, we must, at some point, take the time to consider Derek's thought that Daisy was less important than the greater good of saving the future of thousands of children. However regrettable, the sacrifice of a single child in those circumstances could be argued as a price worth paying. What do you think? On decisions like that rest many consequences and you see how one thing must follow another.

Luckily, by interfering with the natural order Lucy had created an unnatural situation. Placing reaction before action to gain an advantage created the moment where the intended could be revealed. The way it happened was unplanned but the effect would be the same.

Back in Louvain Terrace the family were sitting down to dinner.

Mother shuddered. "It's suddenly gone very cold," she stated.

"Has it?" wondered Father. "I don't feel it."

"Well it has," she said. "I felt it cold like this when the evil woman came here."

Mother looked a little anxious at the memory and continued, "You must have seen all the Spiders walking around recently. They keep themselves to themselves and are no problem, although I must say there were some funny looking ones in various shapes and sizes! Anyway they've all gone. Surely you've noticed?" she said to Father.

"Afraid not, my dear. I leave all that sort of thing to you," he answered.

"I do hope everything's all right with our little Spider," Mother said. "I'm so worried about him."

In the underground hall a voice from the gloom said, "You've got a nerve coming here."

"Not really," said Barry. "You know as well as I do that it's where I am now meant to be, and although I come here with nothing there are times when nothing is a lot."

Barry walked boldly towards the cold. He was living on the edge of extremes; all his Supreme senses were in play. This was the moment time had anticipated.

He recognised the voice and said, "I know who you are and you know what I am. We are together now because The Chronicles wish it; no other reason."

"You are as stupid as the others. Have you learnt nothing?" Lucy asked.

She laughed at Barry. "Look at you, the Supreme Spider of legend for whom we have all waited; eventually you arrive and what happens? You throw everything away by sacrificing yourself to us. It's nearly disappointing, but not quite. What happens in Spider Land when you freeze and perish? The Chronicles will be shown as inadequate and useless – just like you, and without their interference we cannot be beaten. You have been outwitted at every stage; all is now done and there is nothing more to say."

Lucy started to turn and walk away.

The Witches started chanting, "Freeze him, freeze him, freeze him," and it became so cold, colder than the world on the ground has ever seen or imagined. All the Witches concentrated their powers in a spell directed at Barry and he could feel his spirit disappearing, second by agonising second. His final thoughts were of his people-family in Louvain Terrace.

Then it happened. The key to The Chronicles turned and they unlocked; their greatest hidden truth was revealed to Barry. It was the precise instant it was meant to be understood but that fact no longer required understanding because reaction was, for an instant longer, still ahead of action. When Lucy made Barry release all the Revelations, she had ensured the beginning of two options, although only one could complete. The Chronicles would either finalise or the Witches would know more than the Spiders. The possibility of the first depended on Barry; the consequences of the second could not even be contemplated.

The third Unnumbered stated:

"There is something Spiders cannot evolve towards nor understand. It is beyond words and deeds, existing only elsewhere, and is all-powerful. When called upon by others it will sustain and nurture all those given access, even in the most difficult of circumstances."

Barry had previously failed to appreciate the meaning and importance of this particular Unnumbered, but he couldn't do otherwise until the time was right. Whatever the "something" was, it existed "only elsewhere" and so had actually been beyond his understanding. To make it even more complicated it could only be "called upon by others". Yet this was when, in what may have been his last few moments on earth, Barry was given access to a power not found in the world of Spiders, but in the mind of Mother when she was sleeping. He smiled because of the comfort and knowledge finally revealed.

Barry was now part of the essential truth hidden within The Chronicles. All the pages and paragraphs merged into one giant understanding and Revelation; nothing was specific but everything was included. The *Witches Reference Books* could have no reaction.

Only Lucy, as the GCHQ, knew what had happened. She received an overwhelming feeling of wonder just before she saw Barry smile. An unusual shuddering sensation swept through her entire body as she recognised something very different that needed time for consideration. The expression on her face changed and she held up her hand; the chanting stopped, the cold became less intense.

"Wait," she said, "I must think about some new information I have received." She pointed at Barry. "Take him away into the silent cell."

Mary and the other Witches looked astonished that Barry was not to be frozen.

"We have him," Mary said. "Why stop now? This is what we've waited for. After the Supreme, the Supers will have no leadership and no direction. They will be lost and we can prosper."

"Do as I say," Lucy snapped at her. "Then come with me."

A Witch carried the little Spider towards a dark corridor where the silent cell was waiting. It was so called because after entry you were never heard of again, but Lucy was swiftly developing a different plan; things had changed.

An hour or two earlier, back in Louvain Terrace a certain amount of tension had been in the air.

"What do you mean he's gone? Gone where?" Derek wasn't happy.

Martin looked guiltily to one side. "I advised him not to do it, but he's the Supreme, so what could I do? He absolutely insisted that he knew how to find the key to understanding The Chronicles but it rested on placing himself in extreme danger. He's gone underground."

"To the hall?" asked Derek, and Martin nodded.

"Gather up the Supers," Derek commanded. "I'm taking control."

A small army of Super Spiders subsequently marched down the garden path. Derek knew there were ways into the earth through the well-worn trails and tunnels created by ants, although he'd never used them before. Mrs Crier could no longer help and ants don't allow others down there without permission; the Supers weren't Barry.

At the entrance a few soldiers barred their way and demanded to know where they were going. There was no time to spend on undue formalities and so the ants were quickly wrapped up in web-thread and placed in the garden trees, to dangle there until things were sorted. When the trails were too narrow for some of the bigger Spiders to pass through, everyone worked together to widen them. It all took time and there was none to lose but no one would be left behind; that wasn't the way of Supers.

The ant commander Barry had seen earlier now appeared at a junction point and confronted Derek with hundreds of ants behind him, blocking the tunnel path leading further downwards.

"You can't come here," he said.

Derek was thinking that he'd had quite enough of ants, but the Supers were in their territory and some normal rules of good behaviour needed to be followed.

He said, "The Supreme Spider is down there in the Witches' underground hall; he's in great danger and we're on our way to save him. That's all there is to it, so now please get out of our way if you're not going to help."

The ant commander said thoughtfully, "Who would have thought that little Spider was the Supreme, eh? Anyway we know where he is because we said we were ready to help, and we did, but that's nothing to do with you lot. Rules are rules and you other Spiders just can't go wandering around where ever you feel like going. If you wait here I'll see what I can do to get passes underground for everyone, but it may take a little while."

Derek and Martin were at the head of a long trail of Spiders stretching back into the tunnel from where they'd travelled, and after all they were mostly Supers. Derek looked back and decided there was nothing for it but to fight their way through.

"Look, I simply don't have the time to bandy words with you on this; help or get out of the way."

The situation was becoming tense with no obvious answer, but then as if by magic another tunnel appeared leading further downwards and the Spiders charged through before it could be blocked.

Barry had known the Spiders might attempt some sort of rescue mission. He didn't want that; fighting and confrontation are poor solutions to problems. He'd hoped the Supers would have learned more from The Chronicles but it is interesting to note how every creature can perform badly when pressure is applied.

In Mrs Porter's old office, a little way from the underground hall, Lucy was trying to explain things to Mary.

"Listen to me carefully," she said. "Something has changed and everything is different. Not because of the reaction just received but because it is the last reaction. The Chronicles somehow made it travel slowly so it arrived late. It meant I could make the mistake of failing to see that nothing can exist out of turn. Now we must change."

"Why? I see no reason for that," Mary replied. "How do you know this is the last reaction? Spiders receive Revelations and we react to them. It means everything stays in balance and we continue along our path."

Lucy was sounding impatient. "You're wrong. There will be no more reactions, try to understand. In the Great Hall just now Barry was given the key unlocking The Chronicles. He received a Revelation that cannot be explained and so, believe me, this is our last one."

She was pointing at a *Witches Reference Book* lying open on the table. These 50 words were now before them, it was the final and only reaction of that length.

"The time has come when action and reaction are useless, for within the one there is the other and the second cannot be allowed to overtake or become the first. Begin again from a different place because there is no path to safely follow without light to guide the way."

The Missing had all been revealed by Barry some time ago with the following Revelation, Chapter 15 paragraph 152, being the last released. However, the above reaction to it had travelled slowly and reached the *Witches Reference Books* only when the advice it contained could be understood.

"Reaction cannot go before action yet both must find their place, as the second is the first and what was completed by one is finished with the other. Nothing can end before it begins and then there is a different journey where unwritten knowledge becomes the most powerful truth and gives the greatest understanding."

Beneath the next paragraph (a text I have previously provided), an unreferenced sentence had appeared, followed by a Draw line.

Lucy had allowed paragraph 152 and the corresponding update in the *Witches Reference Books* to become possible. It need not have occurred but in placing reaction before action she had overreached herself, like Mrs Porter had done some time previously. You should note there are no new mistakes, only different consequences.

Her interference in what must be expected led to the downfall of the Witches. The Chronicles unlocked to reveal their greatest secret proving why good triumphs over evil. The timing for it required the Supreme to trust in the moment it would happen. The Unnumbered served that single purpose; they could pass through Barry's eyes only and now disappeared.

Lucy realised The Chronicles had confirmed something that couldn't be explained by either Spiders or Witches. She decided it would therefore be unwise to provide any detailed information on matters where their reference books must remain silent.

She told Mary the broadest of outlines. "Until recently the updates we received were always just reactions. They were inadequate because the Spiders gained knowledge sooner than us. Then with the Supreme releasing every Revelation, before many had been understood, I thought at last we had a chance to know more than them through the reactions we would receive. We could enter into the light. However, The Chronicles wouldn't allow it to happen so they interfered with the travelling time of this last reaction, as well as giving extra information and guidance to Barry. With that help he has found and felt a teaching so powerful there is no choice for us but to change; it is the way and not the option. I was wrong to borrow time and reverse a natural order and the result is that we must begin again elsewhere, using the past to guide us better. I had another plan ready to be triggered in Louvain Terrace but no matter, let it be unused."

Every Spider leg was in chains when Lucy came into the silent cell; it was not cold. Barry could doubtless have escaped, but he needed to be sure of a few more things.

Spider and Witch looked at each other for a moment. She said, "I know," and the chains immediately fell away.

"I see that and feel it," answered Barry. Lucy continued, "We cannot stay here so we will leave. It is enough that the great knowledge has been revealed to a Spider. It came to you before we could take advantage of all the reactions. I acted in error to make you release them."

Barry agreed. "Yes, you should not have reversed what must be expected. It forced the key to turn and unlock the biggest truth."

They looked at each other for a moment before Barry continued.

"When you interfered with time, The Chronicles reacted by doing the same thing. They ensured the final update travelled slowly and arrived too late; it was nothing to do with me. Who knows what might otherwise have happened? Now, because there is no response to something that cannot be explained, you must leave."

"There are different places," replied Lucy. "It has been proven before and we will also find somewhere that suits us, perhaps even suits us better. Maybe some magical place underneath the fairy teeth in a land of paper stars **and the ticking tree?** Someone's world becomes another's. Farewell, little Supreme Spider. Return to your family and your kind without hurt nor harm."

As she turned to leave the silent cell Barry couldn't help but ask a question; Spiders are so nosey.

"Wait. What was the alternative plan you had prepared? I knew there was another when you offered to return Daisy. I hadn't wanted to release any Revelations but you left me no choice. The improved protective web around Louvain Terrace meant no new spell could arrive to threaten us so I'd like to know what you intended."

Lucy smiled. "Your web had no influence over any family member or anything that was, or had already been, within Louvain Terrace. There were two sweets inside the parcel I sent Daisy from Spain. The first was hidden in the packaging and the second was inside Rodrigo. When I returned Daisy she brought it back through the web. Both spells were inactive until triggered; one by touch and the other when his eyes turned colour. I knew you would close him down. I have no need of it now so let it be harmless."

For a second or two Lucy seemed to be thinking of another outcome. "Your understanding certainly arrived at the right moment."

"Why? What was that second spell going to do?" asked Barry.

"It isn't the time for you to know," answered Lucy, smiling as she left the cell.

Barry was free. It meant that Spiders were able to live in peace and continue their happy, friendly, useful lives. Most importantly children all over the world could live in safety from Witches.

When Barry returned home Derek and Martin were waiting.

"Barry, is that you? You're not dead?" Derek said in a voice full of relief.

"Not at all," said Barry. "As if…" he stopped to leave the

remark unfinished.

"We tried to reach you. We got all the Supers together and headed down towards the Great Hall but some ants blocked our path. We thought we had found another way down, but every time we followed that path or any path it kept returning us to the surface," Martin tried to explain.

"Yes, well it seemed best to give you something to follow, even if it would lead nowhere. I had already explained that I needed to go underground, alone, before The Chronicles would unlock. You seem to have the selective memory of a fisherman in the things you recall," but Barry laughed, he wasn't angry. He knew how easy it was to remember things that had never happened and forget those that did.

The Spiders had only wanted to do the right thing and there are many times when trying to help achieves the opposite result. Prudent action will always follow informed advice; emotion gets in the way. Barry had allowed himself to be trapped by his feelings where Daisy was concerned but he knew there was not, and never would be, a time to weave spells and plant thoughts beyond the teaching of The Chronicles.

"Sorry, but we want to know," Derek and Martin echoed each other. "What happened down there? All the Revelations you released are no longer underlined and every chapter has a Draw line. Are The Chronicles completed and understood?"

"Yes," answered Barry. "The time came when everything needing to be known was revealed. I just had to find trust that the moment would arrive. There is more to this world than can be understood, so the breaking news is that," and he paused for effect as the Spiders waited expectantly, "all is well."

I mentioned before how The Chronicles concluded with a single unreferenced sentence previously unseen. It was not a Revelation nor part of The Missing because there could be no reaction to something that required no understanding.

Barry had already realised that the best answer to the many questions certain to arise came from within the 14 words now shown. He understood The Chronicles at the moment he knew of something they could never contain.

"What is neither described or explained cannot be told,
so then all is well."

After studying the Revelations, and trying to connect many different paragraphs and meanings, he found that the simplest unwritten truth, existing elsewhere, was the key to everything.

Perhaps it was that a Mother's love is the most powerful force in the world.